"Get away from that

Her attackers froze. They
over their shoulders.

"Get him!" the tall man y

They tossed Sasha aside like a rag doll and charged the man, all three falling back into the hallway with a loud clamor of men knocking against walls and the scuffle of boots.

The blast of gunfire resounded in the hallway, leaving in its wake the pungent scent of gunpowder and smoke. A man cried out. Sasha could only hope it wasn't her champion.

Heart throbbing, she grabbed her reticule, snatched up her satchel, and darted into the hallway, barely missing getting kicked. She glanced at the pile of thrashing bodies, unable to see who had the advantage because of the dimly lit hall and the lingering cloud of smoke. Hurrying toward the rear exit, she fled the frightening commotion.

VICKIE MCDONOUGH believes God is the ultimate designer of romance. She is a wife of thirty-two years, a mother to four sons, and a doting grandma. When not writing, she enjoys reading, watching movies, and traveling. Visit Vickie's Web site at www.vickiemcdonough.com.

Books by Vickie McDonough

HEARTSONG PRESENTS
HP671—Sooner or Later
HP716—Spinning Out of Control
HP731—The Bounty Hunter and the Bride

He that trusteth in his riches shall fall:
but the righteous shall flourish as a branch.

PROVERBS 11:28

A note from the Author:
*I love to hear from my readers! You may correspond with
me by writing:*

Vickie McDonough
Author Relations
PO Box 721
Uhrichsville, OH 44683

ISBN 978-1-59789-510-1

A WEALTH BEYOND RICHES

All scripture quotations are taken from the King James Version of the
Bible.

All of the characters and events in this book are fictitious. Any resem-
blance to actual persons, living or dead, or to actual events is purely
coincidental.

*Our mission is to publish and distribute inspirational products offering
exceptional value and biblical encouragement to the masses.*

PRINTED IN THE U.S.A.

A Wealth Beyond Riches

Vickie McDonough

Heartsong Presents

one

New York City, April 1906

A knock sounded on the door of Sasha Di Carlo's hotel room, and her mother glided inside without even waiting for a "Come in." She eyed Sasha's evening gown, hiked her chin, and sniffed. "There's been a change of plans."

Always one to make a grand entrance, Cybil Di Carlo flipped open her oriental fan and waved it back and forth, fluttering the coal black tendrils of hair around her temples. The lavender silk of her Liberty and Co. evening dress swished back and forth as she moved further into the room. The scent of expensive perfume overpowered the lemony smell of oil the maid had used earlier to polish the furniture.

"What do you mean? What's changed?" Sasha stared at her mother and sucked in her breath as the maid secured the back of her frilly party dress.

Cybil waved her fan at the maid, which sent the dark-skinned servant scurrying out of the hotel room. Her mother lifted her nose in the air with a hint of disinterest. "I know it's your birthday, dear, but Nigel just surprised me with tickets to *The Earl and the Girl*. You know how I've been dying to see the Casino Theater ever since it was rebuilt after the fire. It's all the rage now. I can't disappoint Nigel. Those tickets cost him a fortune and are almost impossible to acquire."

Disbelief clogged Sasha's throat, and tears burned her eyes. Her mother wouldn't dare disappoint her latest beau—a wealthy

Englishman Cybil had known a mere month—but her daughter was another thing. Sasha's frustration bubbled out. "But it's my eighteenth birthday. We've planned this evening for weeks."

"Oh, for heaven's sake, Anastasia, don't be so melodramatic." Cybil clicked her fan shut and eyed Sasha with a narrowed gaze. "You know if Nigel had an extra ticket I would drag you along with us."

Sasha pressed her lips together, doubting Cybil's last statement. Her famous actress mother had never been affectionate, but she had always treated Sasha to a birthday dinner each year. It was a rare, special time that Sasha cherished. One of the few times she was certain to have her popular mother's undivided attention. She closed her eyes and pushed aside her aching disappointment. She wouldn't cry in front of her mother no matter how much her heart hurt. That would only bring a stern reprimand.

"There is more."

With her emotional control tied together by only a thin thread, Sasha composed herself and opened her eyes.

Her mother tugged off her white kid glove, held out her left hand, and smiled. "Nigel asked me to marry him. Don't you just adore the ring he gave me?"

Unable to believe Cybil had finally accepted a man's offer of marriage, Sasha stared at the gaudy diamond ring on her mother's finger. She imagined after wearing the huge stone for a day her mother's wrist would be aching.

"It's—uh. . .large."

Cybil pressed her lips together in a proud gloat. Her gaze caressed the oversized rock. "Yes, it is. Quite. That snooty Thelma Crowley will be green with envy." Her mother's black eyes glinted.

"I suppose congratulations are in order." Sasha couldn't help wondering how this change would affect her. Whenever her mother turned her back when all three were together, Nigel Grantham's leering gaze at Sasha made her shudder. She couldn't stand the man.

Her mother's painted lips tilted up in a sickly sweet smile. "Yes, well, you could be a bit more enthusiastic." While she wrestled her hand back into her glove, Cybil's gaze traveled the room that had been Sasha's home for the past twelve months. "I simply can't fathom why you're happy staying in such quaint quarters."

"I don't need all the space you require, Mother, and it's affordable. Besides, it has the same view of the city as your suite." Sasha stifled a sigh, wondering how her mother could consider any room at the fashionable Castleworth as quaint.

Cybil sashayed over to the chest of drawers and fingered a small statue of the Eiffel Tower. Sasha had picked it up as a souvenir of their two-year stint in Europe, where her mother had acted in several plays while Sasha had worked as a makeup artist. Now they made their home in the Castleworth Hotel where her mother's luxurious suite took up one-fourth of the top floor, while Sasha's more conservative single room was on the third floor.

Though physically she was almost an exact replica of her beautiful mother, on the inside, they were very different. Cybil craved attention and fawning from anyone who was willing, but Sasha only yearned for her mother's love. Now it looked as if she might never achieve that dream.

"I am quitting the theater, darling. Nigel is wealthy enough that I no longer have to work. Instead, I will content myself with sitting in his private theater box seats and being part of the adoring audience. I suppose your salary with Geoffrey's troupe will keep you living in the style you are accustomed to."

Sasha blinked, confusion fogging her brain. "What do you mean?"

Her mother snapped open the fan again. "Anastasia, you are eighteen now. It is past time you were on your own. I will no longer be supporting you."

All manner of emotions assaulted Sasha. Her mother hadn't truly supported her since she was sixteen when Sasha had been hired as the head makeup artist and had also begun serving as her mother's understudy. A measure of fear snaked up her spine. Even though she was already providing for herself, her mother had been there to fall back on if things hadn't gone as planned. Not that it had ever happened.

Still, she couldn't help feeling she was losing something precious—even if it was only her dream.

"Anyway, Nigel is downstairs waiting. I must be off. You and I will catch dinner together another time." Cybil stared at her as if she wanted to say more, then snapped shut her fan and stuffed it in her beaded handbag.

The door clicked shut as Cybil left, and Sasha felt more alone than she ever had. Tears blurred her eyes, but she forced them away. She'd learned long ago how hard-hearted and selfish her mother could be. But her birthday had been the one day she could count on having her mother to herself.

Ignoring the hunger pangs rumbling in her stomach, she wandered over to the window and stared out at the busy traffic on 32nd Avenue. People on their way to dinner, others heading home from work, and still more on their way to theater shows continued on their merry ways, oblivious that her heart had just shattered.

It had taken a lot of effort to persuade her boss, Geoffrey, to allow her and Cybil to have the evening off. Up-and-comer Lorinda Swanson had been only too happy to play the lead role, and fortunately, she was up on all the lines. But all Sasha's efforts had been for naught.

She continued watching the people below. How could someone feel so utterly alone in such a mass of humanity?

Sasha clenched her fist as she remembered her mother's coldhearted glare. The woman didn't care one whit that she'd chosen her new fiancé over her own daughter.

Sasha's satin dress rustled as she crossed the room and flopped onto the bed. All she ever wanted was to belong. To someone. To some place.

Her mother had always considered her a nuisance. Sasha shuddered as she thought of the times as a child when she'd sat quietly alone in the dark of a hotel's wardrobe while her mother entertained her male friends. Sasha had learned to hide in the silky long dresses and pretend she was a fairy princess.

She picked up the Bible on the night table beside the bed. She'd meant to return it to the desk clerk but had forgotten. Some nice organization had donated it to the hotel. She didn't understand everything within the thick book's pages, but certain passages warmed her heart and gave her hope.

At eighteen, she was already tired of the theater, but it was the only life she knew—the only way she could support herself. Unshed tears burned her eyes and made her throat ache. If only she had some clue who her father was—maybe she could go to him. But her mother had always refused to talk about him. Sasha didn't even know his name.

A yawn forced its way out. She'd looked forward to her birthday dinner for weeks, and disappointment weighed heavily upon her. Though it was only 8:00 p.m., Sasha closed her eyes and hugged the Bible to her chest. Maybe tomorrow would be better.

&a

An incessant pounding pulled Sasha from her sleep. She yawned and glanced at the window, noting the sun must have been up several hours. The Ansonia Chamberlain on the fireplace mantel read nine o'clock.

"I'm coming. Just a minute."

She slipped off the bed, padded across the room in her bare feet, and unlocked the door, hoping to see her mother. The theater had been closed on Sunday and Monday, so the last time she'd seen Cybil was that disappointing Saturday evening.

The maid's dark eyes widened. "Mercy me, Miz Di Carlo! For such an early riser, you sho' have been sleeping late these past few days." The young colored woman hurried behind Sasha and flung open the drapes. Sasha squinted, for the bright light hurt her dry, gritty eyes. She'd slept late because it had taken until after 2:00 a.m. to fall asleep the past few nights. Sasha yawned and stretched, wondering if she'd see her mother today.

Prissy opened the wardrobe, revealing the wrinkled, pale green evening dress Sasha had purchased especially for her birthday dinner. She had hoped her appearance in the fancy new gown would please her critical mother, but Cybil hadn't even noticed.

Disappointed again, Sasha removed her nightgown and flopped onto the Victorian sofa, dressed only in her undergarments. Today would be better than yesterday. She'd spent enough time upset, and she needed to put the past behind her.

Prissy rummaged through the wardrobe. "What would you like to wear? Your pale blue day dress? Or perhaps the yellow one?"

Sasha waved her hand in the air. "It doesn't matter. You

pick." Her stomach grumbled, reminding her she hadn't eaten much lately. She'd had little appetite. Breakfast was usually a lonely affair as her mother rarely rose before noon.

Prissy fluffed the yellow gown. "You need something cheery today." She laid the dress on the bed, then pivoted. "Oh, I almost forgot. Your mama gave me a package to give to you. And I have one from the hotel manager, too."

Hope sparked within Sasha. Had her mother perhaps sent her a birthday gift to make up for missing dinner?

Prissy pulled two envelopes from her apron pocket and handed them to her, one bearing the hotel insignia. "I'll just go get some fresh water whilst you read your letters."

The door clicked shut as the maid slipped out. Sasha turned over the thicker, plain white envelope. It didn't look like a present.

Business first, then hopefully pleasure. She loosened the flap on the hotel envelope and pulled out a heavy linen sheet.

Dear Miss Di Carlo,
  We here at the Castleworth Hotel are very sorry to see your mother leave.

As she read the short missive, her heart stumbled. Sasha crinkled her forehead. What was he talking about? Her mother wasn't going anywhere. She still had ten months left on her contract.

  We have enjoyed having you both as our guests this past year. However, I regret that I must inform you that the rate for your room must be increased. We have graciously charged you only half price, due to the fact that your mother was also staying in one of our top-floor suites. Now that that is no

longer the case, we must charge you full price for your room.
The rate increase goes into effect beginning Monday.

She lowered the letter to her lap, trying to make sense of it.
If she had to pay full price, she would be forced to find a room
in a less expensive hotel. But what was all this chatter about
her mother leaving?

With shaking hands, she picked up her mother's thick envelope, loosened the flap, and peered inside. There was a folded
sheet of what looked like hotel stationery and a yellowed
envelope. She pulled out the paper, and a pile of money fell
into her lap. Curious, she read the note.

Sasha darling,
 By the time you read this letter, Nigel and I will have
departed for England. He persuaded Geoffrey to release me
from my contract, and we are getting married at Grantham
Manor, his family's two-hundred-year-old castle. This will
come as a shock, but you are a capable girl and will be fine
without me.
 I know you have been curious about your heritage. You
certainly needled me enough with endless questions about it.
I must confess that my past is a grievance to me. I couldn't
bear to voice the horrible truth out loud. You will understand
when you read the enclosed letter. I will see you on our return
in a year or two.

Thinking of you,
Cybil Angelina Di Carlo

Stunned, Sasha stared at the letter. Her mother was gone?
To England?

Cybil must have planned this for weeks. She couldn't simply

secure passage on a ship so quickly. Her mother hadn't even had the nerve to tell her good-bye in person. Sasha pressed her hand against her aching heart. She thought nothing could feel worse than the pain she'd encountered on her birthday, but she'd been mistaken.

She wadded up the letter and tossed it across the room, then grabbed the dollars, slinging them aside, and watched as they spiraled down to the carpet. Penance money—that's what it was. Money to ease her mother's guilty conscience.

Pressing her lips tightly together, she locked her hands in her lap to keep them from trembling.

"Am I so worthless my own mother doesn't want me?"

Cybil hadn't even had faith that her daughter could take care of herself and had to shame her by giving her money. She hadn't even signed the letter with "Mother," but instead used her full name.

Well, she was truly on her own now. Sighing, Sasha took hold of the aged envelope and turned it in her hands. The letter was from a Dewey Hummingbird in Indian Territory. She closed her eyes and searched her memory to see if that name held some meaning.

No, she'd never heard it before.

The yellowed envelope crackled as she withdrew the paper from inside. An unfamiliar scribbling covered several pages. Sasha rubbed her eyes and began reading.

Dearest Myrtle,

Myrtle? She glanced at the envelope again. *Who is Myrtle?* Only one way to find out, so she continued reading.

Or should I call you by your theater name—Cybil? How

*I long to see you again. I hope you and Anastasia are well.
Your aunt Kizzie married Raymond Arbuckle and is living
on the land next to mine. They are very happy and would
love to have a whole tribe of children, but Kizzie has been
unable to become with child. My Jenny is gone now. Buried
her last August under the big oak on the hill behind my
cabin.*

*I wish you and Sasha could come visit. How old is she
now? Three? Four?*

Sasha laid the letter in her lap. Confusion swirled with
excitement. She had family! An aunt and this man who wrote the
letter. But how could her mother have kept this correspondence
for nearly fifteen years and never have mentioned it?

*I feel I should have done more to make you happy, but you
were never the same after your parents were killed. I know
living on a farm in Indian Territory was hard for you. You
always had such big dreams. Forgive me for my shortcomings.
And please, if you find the time, come and bring your
daughter for a visit. She deserves the chance to meet her
Creek relatives and to learn about her rich ancestry.*

*Always yours,
Your uncle, Dewey Hummingbird
Creek Nation, Indian Territory*

*P.S. Things have greatly changed around here, so I've included
directions to my home, in case you decide to visit.*

Numb, Sasha stared out the window across the room. She'd
always dreamed of and longed for a heritage, but to be an
Indian! People in New York referred to Indians as savages.

Was it true?

The man in the letter sure didn't sound like a savage. He could even read and write.

Did her mother never tell her about their Indian heritage because she was ashamed? Or because she thought people would treat her unkindly? She must have been ashamed since she'd changed her name and had kept the information a secret all these years.

Sasha closed her eyes, trying to take it all in. All her life she'd thought she was Italian because of their last name. Was Di Carlo her father's surname—or just another name her mother had made up?

Being Indian also explained her mother's high cheek bones and black hair and eyes. Sasha crossed the room and stared in the mirror. Her facial features were similar to her mother's, but her complexion and hair color were quite a bit lighter.

What would her friends say if they knew she was Indian?

What about Geoffrey, her employer?

Now she understood the secret burden her mother had borne all these years. Myrtle Hummingbird must have left home, changed her name, and become an actress.

All her life Sasha had wanted to belong to a family and to settle down and live in a real house. For as long as she could remember, she wanted to quit living in hotels and have a place to put down roots. To be accepted for whom she was on the inside, not because she was pretty or had a famous mother.

But to be an Indian—a half-breed, most likely—was more than she could comprehend. Would the theater troupe members despise her if they learned the truth?

She looked down at the letter in her fist. It was the only link to her family. Pressing the paper against her lap, she smoothed it. Somewhere, far away in Indian Territory, she had a relative—an uncle who wanted to meet her.

Sasha glanced at the money strewn across her floor. Was there enough to get her to Indian Territory and back? Would Geoffrey allow her to take a leave of absence from the theater, especially since her mother had just left?

Or maybe she should quit. There were plenty who could take her place.

Then again, if they learned she was part Indian, they might boot her out of the troupe without even a second glance. She and her mother would most likely become pariahs.

But she had family—family who longed to see her.

She paced the room, wrestling with her discovery. Should she go to Indian Territory and meet her uncle and learn of her heritage? Or should she stay in New York and live a lie, doing a job that didn't hold her heart?

She had toured the richest cities of eastern America and Europe with her mother and other members of the acting troupe, but did she dare travel west—far past Chicago—to primitive Indian Territory?

With a quick knock, Prissy slipped back into the room and eyed the money on the floor. Having worked several years at the hotel, she ignored the scene and set her bucket of water beside the basin. "You ready to wash up, ma'am?"

Sasha nodded. "Did you know my mother was leaving, Prissy?"

The maid ducked her head and fiddled with her apron. "Yes'm, but Miz Cybil threatened to have me fired if I said a word. I'm so sorry, Miz Sasha."

"It's all right. I understand."

"Pardon me for saying, but your mama is jealous of you."

Sasha's head jerked up. "Jealous? Of me? Why ever for?"

"You're prettier than her. She's afraid you'd soon steal the lead from her, and she couldn't handle that thought, so she done run off."

Sasha blinked in disbelief. Was that truly what her mother thought? That she'd try to take her place? The thought had never even entered Sasha's mind and only emphasized how little Sasha knew her own mother.

Pushing aside her disappointment, Sasha allowed an excitement that she hadn't felt in a long time to surge through her. She had family. Family who wanted to meet her.

She spun around. "Yes, I want to wash up, and then I need you to help me pack."

Prissy blinked in confusion. "But your mama's already gone. It's too late to join her."

A grin tugged at Sasha's lips. "I'm not going with Mother. I'm going to visit my uncle."

two

Creek Nation, Indian Territory, May 1906

Sasha stared out the window of the gently swaying train, wondering how much longer it would be before she arrived in Tulsa. They had already crossed into Indian Territory, but she'd yet to see a tepee or an Indian out the window. Though many of the passengers looked as if they might carry Native American blood, their clothing seemed nearly as modern as her own.

Still, she couldn't stop the chills that charged up her spine. Did Indians still go on the warpath?

She'd heard stories of pioneers meeting up with bands of renegade Indians who shot zinging arrows and whooped eerie cries. Some adventurers had even lost their scalps and lives. She shuddered and reached up, tugging her hat forward, hoping and praying those days were past.

But then, she was of Indian blood. A half-breed most likely. Would that make any difference if the train were attacked?

A man across from her cleared his throat, and Sasha jumped.

"I was wondering, ma'am, would you do me the honor of accompanying me to dinner at our next stop? I'm rather tired of the dining car's food and fancy something different."

She stifled a sigh and stared at the gentleman dressed stylishly in his gray three-piece suit. Hope sparked in his pale blue eyes. He ran a neatly manicured finger over his thin moustache.

She'd lost count of the number of men who had offered to buy her meals and pushed their unwanted attentions her way since she'd left New York. A few men had even asked her to marry them. She now understood why most women traveled with an escort. But for her, that hadn't been an option.

It had been a mistake to dress in her tailored Edwardian suit. The short bolero jacket only helped to emphasize her narrow waist, but the dark blue color was perfect for traveling because it didn't show dirt or coal dust.

She glanced at the man, patiently awaiting her response. "I sincerely appreciate your kindness, sir, but I do not intend to disembark the train for dinner at our next stop." No, but she would locate her trunk and fetch a change of clothing.

"But surely you must eat." He leaned forward, resting his elbows on his knees.

Oh, how she wished these train seats didn't face one another. She shook her head. "Thank you, but I have something leftover from my last stop."

He pressed his lips together and sat back. "As you wish."

Relieved that he acquiesced, Sasha focused her attention on the passing landscape again. Growing up the daughter of a famous and beautiful actress, she'd had her share of men's attentions. Though her mother craved the limelight and being fawned over by adoring men, Sasha had never liked it. Somehow she felt there had to be more to a relationship between a man and a woman than physical attraction. She longed for friendship and even love. But she'd seen few examples in the theater world of happily married couples.

Sasha could feel the man across from her staring, and she sighed, wishing she'd worn her old woman's costume. When things in New York became more than she could bear, she'd skillfully apply some theater makeup and dress as an old woman. Incognito, she was free to ramble the streets of New York without an escort or sit in a park without disturbance.

Her old woman's costume had served her well and had given her the freedom to wander where she wanted without drawing the attention of half the men on the street.

A half hour later, the train stopped in a small town that resembled ten others they'd passed through. In the washroom of the depot, Sasha changed out of her travel clothes and put on her costume that a kind freight conductor had helped her retrieve from her trunk. Now she shuffled down the aisle, dressed as an elderly woman. Her cane tapped out a slow rhythm as she made her way to the final seat, which faced the wall of the train. Her makeup was good at a distance but most likely wouldn't hold up to close scrutiny.

As she settled herself on the wooden seat, she set her cane on the bench beside her to discourage anyone from sitting there. She readjusted her fringed scarf and stared out the window with a smile tugging at her lips. Several men, including the one who'd asked her to dinner, had looked her way and tipped their hats, but not a one had pressed his attentions. Perhaps she'd have solitude for the final leg of her long trip.

From her satchel, she dug out a hard biscuit left over from breakfast, as she eagerly anticipated her arrival. What would her uncle think when he finally saw her?

She'd left New York so quickly that she hadn't taken time to write a letter or send him a telegraph message. Would he be happy to see her?

Mile after mile of low hills and wild acres of tall prairie grass sped by. The gently rolling landscape was refreshing after the flat, treeless plains of Kansas.

Her thoughts drifted back to the big buildings of New York. Would she ever return? She wasn't sure that she wanted to. Deep in her heart, she hoped that she'd find the family she'd always longed for. But she hadn't yet reconciled herself to the fact that she was part Indian—Creek Indian.

What would her theater troupe say if they learned the truth? What would life be like in an Indian village? Was it possible that her uncle live in a tepee?

She had so many questions and nobody to answer them.

The train slowed as it made a sluggish turn to the south. Gradually it began to pick up speed again, and the gentle swaying lulled Sasha into a relaxed state. She closed her eyes and saw a picture of her mother. Had Cybil missed her yet?

A more poignant question was, did she miss her mother?

An ache coursed through her as she realized she did. If she stayed in Indian Territory, she'd probably never see Cybil again, and that thought made her sad, in spite of the way her mother had treated her. They'd never been close, and Cybil had made it clear on many occasions how inconvenient it was to be a famous celebrity and have to deal with the responsibility of a child. Sasha had grown up quickly and learned to depend on herself. Still, as long as her mother was around, she had never been totally alone. Until now. Unshed tears burned her eyes, and her throat tightened.

Please, Uncle Dewey. . .please want me.

❧

Two hours later, Sasha retied her scarf and picked up her satchel and handbag. There was definitely a negative side to dressing like an old woman. She'd already stopped at five of the nicer Tulsa hotels and several of the lower-class ones that people here referred to as "cowboy hotels." Each clerk had refused to rent her a room, saying, "We don't rent to Gypsies."

She'd never even seen a Gypsy before and had no idea that her costume resembled one until now.

Sasha looked ahead and to her left to make sure no one was watching, then darted down a dark alley. Her heart pounded, and she prayed she wouldn't run into any Indians, not that the ones she'd seen so far looked all that fierce. In fact, much to her surprise, most resembled white men with just darker skin and hair. Very few had been dressed in what she assumed was native garb. Most of the hotel clerks had even looked like they were of Indian blood.

She found an unlocked shed behind the Whitaker Hotel and scurried into it. Leaning against the closed door, she willed her heart to slow its frantic pace. Things were so different here in Tulsa. The handful of buildings were only a few stories high, and everything seemed so rustic. The town was so small compared to New York City. She could only hope she was doing the right thing by coming here.

Changing clothes quickly, she considered what the clerk at the train depot had told her. After she had made arrangements to store her trunk until she could return for it, the clerk confirmed that Dewey Hummingbird used to live in Keaton, near where oil was first found at the Glenn Pool strike. The man knew her uncle because Dewey had occasionally picked up freight at the Tulsa depot, but the clerk hadn't seen him in a long time. Disappointment surged through her. Traveling across the country and buying frequent meals had cost more than she'd expected. With her funds dwindling, what would she do if her uncle no longer lived in the area?

As she entered the Whitaker Hotel, again dressed in her stylish travel clothes and with her makeup removed, she noticed the clerk's gaze rivet on her. His eyes sparked, and he straightened his black vest and string tie. A man on her side of the counter also turned to stare, a leering grin tilting his cheek.

"Howdy, ma'am. What can I help you with?" The clerk's interested gaze darted sideways toward his buddy, and he lifted his eyebrows up and down.

Sasha never ceased to be amazed at how men could be so easily swayed by a pretty woman. No one had shown kindness to her when she was dressed as an old woman. Was there not a single man in the world who had character?

Lifting her chin, she pinned the clerk with a stern glare. "I'd like a room for the night, please."

He adjusted his string tie again and cleared his throat. "I'd be happy to rent you a room, but mostly cowpokes and oil workers bunk here. Wouldn't you be more comfortable in a fancier hotel?"

Sasha shook her head. "I've already been told there are no rooms available at those establishments."

"Well. . ." The man leaned on the counter and narrowed his eyes, "I have a room, but I can't guarantee your safety. We don't often get women traveling alone here—at least not of your caliber. If you know what I mean."

Sasha surmised what he meant but didn't want to think about the ladies of the night. "I assure you I'm quite able to take care of myself. So, if you don't mind, I've traveled a long ways and am rather tired."

"Suit yourself." He shrugged one shoulder, pushed the registration book toward her, and collected her coins.

She followed him up the stairs of the bare, wooden structure and down a dimly lit hallway toward two rugged cowboys. Their low rumbling voices halted as she drew near. One man leaned against the door jamb, and the other stood in the narrow walkway. Whiskers shaded their jaws, and they smelled strongly of cigars and cattle.

"Whoowee! Would you look at that, Sam. A real lady, right here at Whitaker's."

Sasha hugged the wall and hurried closer to the clerk as she passed the men.

"Mmm-mmm. Sure does make your mouth water." The taller of the two men sidestepped and blocked her path. "H'lo there, missy."

Sasha halted and shivered as the second man sidled up behind her. She'd had her share of run-ins with dandies in New York. These men might dress and smell differently, but they were all the same. Stroke their egos, and you could usually get what you wanted—that was one thing she'd learned from her mother. As she formulated her words, she heard footsteps stomping toward her.

"You two leave that woman be. She's a customer just like you. If you cause trouble, you'll be out on the streets." The clerk glared at the two men.

One cowboy smirked, his gray eyes burning holes into her. "I think you're wrong, Dwight. She ain't nothing like me." He tipped his hat, and the floor squeaked as he stepped aside. "Be seeing you later, ma'am."

The clerk opened a door several rooms past the cowboys and handed her a key. "I try to run a clean place, but with all the rough cowpokes and roustabouts who stay here, it's difficult. I'll bring up some fresh water. And I don't have to tell you to stay in your room and keep the door locked, do I?"

Sasha shook her head and hurried inside, closing and securing the door. She looked around the sparse room, so different from the nice one she'd had in New York. The bare, unpainted walls reeked of cigar smoke. The bed was simply a plain, wooden frame with a sagging mattress and worn quilt. No carpet decorated the bare, dusty floor. She dragged the ladder-back chair across the tiny room and wedged the top slat under the door handle.

As she dropped her satchel on the narrow bed, her throat tightened. Had she made a horrible mistake coming here?

Tulsa was so rugged, even though the effects of the recent oil boom were evident. Many of the buildings still smelled of fresh wood, and there were several new brick structures. As she'd strolled down the boardwalk, she could hear the sound of hammering in all directions. But everything was so unlike New York. Even the town's odor was different—more like animals and dirt.

Sasha lifted up the lone window and peered out, watching the people wandering along the boardwalk. Though it was still chilly in New York, a stiff, warm breeze blew in her window, lessening the cigar odor.

Having used nearly all of her money to get here, going back would prove difficult. Her training as a makeup artist and intern actress wasn't likely to do her any good in Indian Territory. Besides, she wasn't even sure she wanted to work in theater anymore.

A tear slipped down her cheek. Her throat burned. In New York she never cried, but this was a world away. And her mother wasn't here to chastise her.

Maybe just this once she'd give in to her tears.

&

Jim Conners kicked open the door of his hotel room, removed his hat, and tossed it onto the bed. He crossed the tiny room, pushed aside the dingy curtain, and stared down onto Second Street, watching the people.

He hadn't wanted to overnight in town, but when the load of freight he was supposed to pick up hadn't arrived, he'd had no choice. It was too late to drive back to Keaton today and too dangerous to camp out with all the rough oil workers in the area looking for some nighttime fun. Jim heaved a sigh. He hoped his employer wouldn't worry about him.

A raucous laugh across the hall pulled him from his musing.

"She's a looker, that one. I say we see if she wants some company."

Jim tossed his hat on the bed and looked through his open door across the hall where two men in room four were talking. One man rubbed the back of his neck.

"Yeah, she's a fine lady, but you heard Whitaker—he said he don't want no trouble."

Sensing something was amiss, Jim slipped behind his open door and peered at the men through the crack between the door and the frame.

"Whitaker's downstairs." The shorter man leaned forward toward his friend and spoke softly. "What he don't know, he cain't object to."

A sickening grin tugged the second man's lips, and he cackled a raspy laugh. "You're right, Shorty." He nudged his buddy in the shoulder with his elbow. "I say let's have us some fun. Shhh, here comes Whitaker."

Jim's skin crawled. These two were up to no good, and he suspected an innocent woman would pay the price. Though he had a hankering to head over to the café and get some supper before the place closed, he needed to find out what these two rabble-rousers were up to. If his sister, Katie, ever encountered trouble, he'd like to think someone would help her. How could he do any less?

Jim heard footsteps treading down the wooden hall in his direction. They passed by, and a knock sounded several rooms away.

"I've brung your water, ma'am. I've got customers waiting downstairs, so I'll just leave it here outside your door."

Footsteps rushed in his direction, passed by again, then faded away.

For a few seconds, nothing could be heard except the muffled sounds of outside noises—the whinny of a horse, a faint hint of laughter.

"Dwight's gone, and no one else is around. Now's as good a time as any," the tall man across the hall whispered. "Let's just wait outside her door until she opens it for the water."

"Yeah. Sounds good to me."

The men's spurs jingled as they shuffled into the hall toward the back of the hotel. Jim slipped around the door and peeked out, watching the shorter man's back move away from him. He checked his gun, making sure it was fully loaded, and waited.

In a few seconds, Jim heard the click of a lock and the squeak of a door opening. A woman's brief squeal erupted, followed by a ruckus and the thunk of a bucket being kicked.

Jim sprang into action. He wouldn't stand by and let an innocent woman get hurt, not when he could prevent it.

three

Sasha wrestled her two attackers, smacking one across the nose with her hair brush. He howled and grabbed her right arm. The shorter man struggled to keep his grasp tight on her other arm as she tried hard to claw him with her fingernails. Her heart pounded like a frantic animal's fighting to escape a snare. Bile burned her throat as her fear surged. Never had she been so afraid.

She jerked and struggled, but they were too strong for her. Her worst fears were becoming a reality, and there was no one to help her. Oh, why had she come to this wretched place?

Not yet ready to give up the fight, she kicked one man in the shin, making him curse. Her heart plummeted when another man rushed into the room.

For a brief second, their gazes collided, and she knew instantly when she looked into those brilliant black eyes that help had arrived. He was taller than her captors and broader across the shoulders. The handsome cowboy raised his gun as the two men shoved her up against the wall, oblivious to the third man's presence. Their rank breath and evil glares made her feel faint, but she maintained her focus on her rescuer.

"Now we'll have some fun—"

The cowboy pointed his pistol at them. "Get away from that woman."

Her attackers froze. They glanced at each other, then looked over their shoulders.

"Get him!" the tall man yelled.

They tossed Sasha aside like a rag doll and charged the man, all three falling back into the hallway with a loud clamor of men knocking against walls and the scuffle of boots.

The blast of gunfire resounded in the hallway, leaving in its wake the pungent scent of gunpowder and smoke. A man cried out. Sasha could only hope it wasn't her champion.

Heart throbbing, she grabbed her handbag, snatched up her satchel, and darted into the hallway, barely missing getting kicked. She glanced at the pile of thrashing bodies, unable to see who had the advantage because of the dimly lit hall and the lingering cloud of smoke. Hurrying toward the rear exit, she fled the frightening commotion.

Behind her someone yelled, "Get the sheriff—and the doc. Looks like one of 'em is shot."

At least her rescuer had help now. She dearly hoped he hadn't gotten shot or injured.

Sasha's stampeding heart outpaced her feet as she rushed down the stairs and out into the growing dusk. She hated abandoning her rescuer, but she had to get away. If the cowboy wasn't successful in fighting her two attackers, then surely they'd come after her again.

She dreaded being outside at night, not knowing what she would face. At least in New York City, she knew her way around and knew which places were safe and which weren't. But Indian Territory was as new to her as a script she was reading for the first time.

Ducking behind a toolshed, she took a moment to catch her breath. She pressed her hand to her chest and willed her heart to slow its frantic pace as she peered around the corner. A man ran out the back of Whitaker's Hotel. Sasha held her breath. The faint light of the open door illuminated his back, but his face remained in the shadows.

"Miss? Are you out there?" He leaned his hands on the porch railings and stared into the darkness. "It's safe to come back.

Those two fellows are tied up, and Mr. Whitaker's gone to fetch the sheriff. They won't bother you anymore."

She recognized the blue plaid shirt as belonging to the man who had helped her, and for a brief second, Sasha considered returning to her room. It wasn't much, but it was paid for and better than sleeping outside with the unfamiliar. But if she could be accosted after only being at the hotel a few minutes, how would she manage staying safe overnight? No, she wasn't going back. Hesitating, she wondered if she should thank him. But she wasn't sure whether to trust him or not. When he stepped back inside, she inhaled a deep breath, feeling both guilty and relieved.

She needed to don her costume to feel safe. Nobody would bother an old woman.

☙

Jim clucked to the horses pulling the heavy wagon. This area was his favorite part of the drive from Tulsa to Keaton. The sandy Arkansas River meandered along on his right, and on his left, farm and ranch land rolled on as far as he could see. He was glad that Tulsa didn't allow drilling within the city limits. Oil might make a few folks wealthy beyond their imaginations, but drilling destroyed the beauty of the land.

He sighed and allowed his mind to drift back to last night's events. The vision of the lovely woman he'd glimpsed invaded his thoughts again. Before his scuffle with the two men at the hotel, he'd made split-second eye contact with the frightened lady. He didn't think he'd ever encountered such a lovely woman. She reminded him of a cross between his sister's porcelain doll and a corralled mustang, with her saddle brown mane that hung in soft waves to her waist and brown eyes that had glistened with fear and anger. She'd wielded that hairbrush like a warrior.

By the time he'd knocked both men out cold, the woman

had skedaddled. He'd tried to find her last night but had no luck, and he had hoped to see her this morning at breakfast but was disappointed. He watched for her as he loaded his wagon and drove out of town but had failed to find her.

Who was she? And why was she staying at a seedy place like Whitaker's?

Jim swatted a fly and pulled down his brim to shade his eyes. He'd be happy when the railroad was opened up to Keaton so he wouldn't have to drive the slow-moving wagon clear to Tulsa. The track had been laid, but service wasn't due to start for another week.

Up ahead, he saw someone shuffling down the road. A woman. From her slumped back and grandma-style dress, he suspected she must be quite old. She lugged a satchel in one hand and leaned heavily on a knobby stick, which she used as a cane.

Where in the world was she going? It was at least twelve miles to the Glenn Pool and even further to Keaton.

As the horses pulled even with her, Jim tugged them to a stop and stood. The animals pawed the ground and snorted, as if they knew it wasn't quitting time yet.

"Mornin', ma'am. Can I offer you a ride?"

The woman glanced his way, shook her head, and kept walking.

He didn't blame her for being apprehensive, but he was the last person she needed to fear. Clucking the horses forward, he sat down, drove twenty feet, and then stopped again.

"I don't mean to bother you, ma'am, but it's a good twelve miles to the next town. And with all the oil riffraff in these parts. . . Well, a woman shouldn't travel without an escort."

At those words, she stopped and turned toward him but kept her eyes on the ground.

"Would you mind telling me where you're going?" Jim slid

his hat back on his head and watched as she wrestled her carpetbag.

"Keaton," she muttered.

"Keaton! Well, that's a good fifteen miles or more. You won't make it before dark if you walk, and you definitely don't want to be out alone after the sun sets. Not on this road."

She glanced up. Something sparked in her dark eyes, and she looked away again. After a few moments, she turned toward the wagon but kept her face to the ground. "All right, if you're sure you don't mind, I'll ride with you."

"No, ma'am. I don't mind at all." His boots thumped the ground as he jumped down, stirring up a cloud of dust. He set her satchel in the back and helped her up onto the seat, noticing she seemed rather spry for an old woman as she shinnied up the wheel. She was as thin as a sapling, though.

The wagon creaked as he sat on the seat beside her. Leaving a decent gap in between them, he picked up the reins and nudged his canteen with his boot. "There's water if you're thirsty."

She glanced down, then at him, and leaned forward, picking up the canteen. "Thank you." She drank deeply, then laid the container back on the floor.

He clucked the horses forward, wondering where the woman had come from. She looked a bit like a Gypsy, but her accent was different and her speech sounded as if she might even be an educated woman. In fact, her voice didn't sound half as old as she looked.

"My name's Jim Conners." He glanced sideways, hoping for a peek at her face. "Nice day, isn't it?"

"Mmm."

"Where do you hail from?"

"Back east."

He wasn't much of a talker himself and could take a hint.

This woman was in no mood for conversation. Well, he knew what it was like not to want someone to poke a nose into his business.

He glanced down, and his gaze landed on the woman's hand, which held her scarf tight under her chin. Surprise surged through him. This hand wasn't the wrinkled, withered limb he'd expected to see. It looked as if it belonged to a young woman—a woman with medium brown skin.

Curiosity just about did him in, but he held his tongue. What did he know of old women's hands? He focused his attention on the road. Soon he'd be back at the ranch and would need to get the wagon unloaded.

He glanced at the woman again, but now her hands rested in her lap, hidden under the folds of her skirt. Jim peeked at her face but could only see the side of her scarf and wisps of brown hair, not the gray he'd expected.

She didn't want to talk or let him see her face. Yep, she definitely had something to hide, but it was none of his business.

The driver looked to his left, and Sasha peeked out the corner of her eye. It was him, she was certain—the man who'd come to her rescue last night. And now he was helping her again. She turned her head to the right, just as he faced forward again.

Used to long walks in New York, she hadn't expected the journey to her uncle's home to take so long and was grateful for the ride. It would probably have taken her two full days to walk it, and she hadn't looked forward to spending another night outside.

But would this man see through her makeup? Would he recognize her?

Right after sunup, she'd applied her makeup, using her reflection in a window in lieu of a mirror. She'd tried her best to avoid letting the man look at her face. Though she was an expert in applying stage makeup, it was meant to be viewed at a distance, not close quarters.

She considered the man's kindness to her—once when she was dressed as herself and now as an old woman. She owed him her gratitude and wished that she could thank him. Perhaps there were kind people in Indian Territory after all.

He was a nice-looking man, with his black hair and eyes. She couldn't help wondering if he, too, was part Indian. His skin didn't have the reddish tint that some of the men in Tulsa had but rather was a healthy tanned shade and far more appealing than the pale skin of city men.

They rode along in companionable silence. Sasha studied the countryside, which ranged from gently rolling hills to flatlands where she could see clear to the horizon. Instead of being afraid of the open spaces, she loved the feeling of freedom that came from not being surrounded by New York's lofty buildings and hordes of people.

A gentle breeze teased her face, making her hold on to her scarf so it wouldn't blow off. She'd love nothing more than to allow her hair to blow free like her spirit, but she couldn't. Not yet, anyway.

She fought back a yawn. The warm sun, gentle plodding of hooves, and lack of sleep the night before lulled her into a relaxed state.

❧

Several hours past noon, Mr. Conners gently nudged her arm with his elbow. He nodded his chin forward, and she pushed aside her sleepiness to stare at the changed landscape. She had to physically keep her jaw from dropping.

Tall wooden oil derricks stood out like sentinels everywhere she looked, blotching the landscape. Not a single tree was left standing, but numerous stumps testified that they once had.

Ahead and to her right, the sun shimmered on a lake of some kind of greasy, greenish-black substance.

"This whole area is the Glenn Pool. The Ida Glenn Number One was the first oil strike in these parts. Early last year this was just a cornfield and prairie grass, but now. . .well, you can see for yourself."

Sasha lifted her hand to her nose. "What's that smell?"

"Crude oil. Rather pungent, isn't it?" His smile brightened his whole face, making him look far too handsome for his own good. "Takes a while to get used to."

Holding her scarf over her nose, Sasha stared with amazement at the lake of glimmering substance. "So, is that where the oil comes from? A lake like that?"

Mr. Conners chuckled. "The oilmen wish it was that easy. These lakes of oil are actually overflows. Drillers are bringing in the oil faster than storage tanks can be built, so they resorted to building these earthen dams to hold the excess runoff."

As they drove through the oil field, Sasha watched grimy men scurrying around the tall derricks and working on pumps. The earth here was blackened from the oil, and nothing grew except a few sprigs of grass and obstinate wildflowers. She'd heard that the oil boom had made many people wealthy, but it saddened her to see the landscape ruined.

"That's Rag Town, where many of the oil workers live." He pointed at what looked like a city of tents.

Barefoot children ran around whooping and chasing one another while a tired-looking woman hung ragged clothing on a line. Even the cheap hotel room she'd been in yesterday was far better than this. She couldn't imagine living in such squalor.

"Politicians call the oil boom the next great land rush—a run for riches, a run for power, and a run for national security, but as you can see, very few people here are prospering from it."

She considered his words for a time as they continued their journey. Soon the small town of Keaton came into view. Her heart thudded. She'd hoped that the town her uncle lived near would have some amenities, but its mud streets and rough wooden buildings were a far cry from even Tulsa.

Mr. Conners pulled to a stop. "You sure I can't take you all the way to your destination?"

Sasha shook her head. "No, thank you." She'd used this man enough and could easily get dependent on someone as nice as Jim Conners. She'd learned at a young age that depending on others only brought disappointment. She was a grown woman now, and as her mother said, she needed to take care of herself.

A shiver of apprehension wafted through her as he helped her to the ground. With a trembling hand, she took her satchel from him, thanked him, and said good-bye. He shook the reins, and the wagon pulled away with a soft creak. She breathed a sigh of relief. He was curious about her but hadn't pressed her for information. She thought too late that she should have asked if he knew her uncle.

She studied the people walking up and down the boardwalk. Could one of these men be Dewey Hummingbird? He had to be fairly old now, since he was her mother's uncle.

Her gaze landed on a mortician's shop where a casket leaned up against the wall. Several men were laughing and taking turns standing inside its wooden frame. A horrible thought darted through her mind, and she stumbled on a rut in the road. She took three quick steps to right herself.

What if her uncle were no longer alive? Could she have come all this way for nothing?

four

Jim tightened the cinch and mounted his horse. He'd unloaded the wagon and worked all afternoon but still couldn't get the old woman off his mind. Things just didn't add up. Her voice and hands didn't match her age and face, not that he'd gotten a good peek at her features. And when he had glanced at her, it was her brown eyes that stood out—glimmering with curiosity, but also guarded.

He'd never been acquainted with an elderly woman beyond polite greetings. His mother died when he was six, and he'd never known his grandparents. An overwhelming urge to make sure the old woman was all right had him heading back to Keaton instead of spending an hour reading before bed like he normally did. He nudged his horse forward into a gallop.

An hour later, Jim sighed as he marveled at the pink and orange sunset. The woman was nowhere to be found. He rubbed his hand across his bristly cheek and turned his horse back toward the ranch where he worked, praying the lady found shelter for the night. In May, nights in Oklahoma were usually mild, but no woman should be on the streets alone with all the riffraff around, especially an elderly one. He asked God to watch over her and keep her safe. Maybe he'd have better luck finding her tomorrow, not that he knew what he'd do if he did.

❧

Sasha attempted to smooth the wrinkles from her dress, but it was useless. Too long scrunched up in her satchel, the poor garment needed a good ironing. A half hour ago, she'd slipped off the dirt road and stopped at a stream to refresh herself and change out of her costume. Now, excitement at seeing her uncle battled anxiety as she stared through the growing darkness at the silhouette of his cabin. A lone light in the window beckoned her.

Nearby, a night creature screeched, and Sasha jumped. Darting forward, she raced toward the cabin and onto the porch, pressing her palm to her chest. She'd never been easily spooked, but all these strange noises of nature were new to her and vastly different than those of a big city. Her recent experience at the Whitaker Hotel and Mr. Conners' warnings about not being out at night still lingered in her mind.

Just walking along the dirt road in the daylight had made her legs tremble, but now that the sun had set and who-knew-what was out prowling in the woods. . . Well, she could only hope her uncle would be happy to see her. She didn't want to think what she'd do if he turned her out. At least she'd learned in town that he was still living when she'd asked for directions to his place. With all the new growth because of the oil strike, she'd found her uncle's map almost useless.

The porch's wooden floor creaked, and she lifted her hand to knock.

"Who's out there?"

She jumped at the sound of a man's voice coming from behind the door and licked her lips. "I'm, uh. . .looking for Dewey Hummingbird. Is this his cabin?"

The door opened a crack, and the barrel of a rifle slipped through the opening, pointing straight at Sasha's chest. Her heart skipped a beat.

"Who are you and what do you want at this hour?"

Oh, if only she hadn't been so hasty to leave New York, but

it was too late to succumb to her doubts. She took a deep, straightening breath. "My name is Anastasia Di Carlo, and I'm looking for my uncle, Dewey Hummingbird. Is this the right place?"

She was certain she heard a gasp on the other side of the door. The rifle quickly disappeared, and the door opened, revealing a thin, elderly man. He studied her for a moment, then his mouth broke into a smile, revealing several missing teeth.

"I can't believe it!" He slapped his leg several times, looked past her, and then back. "How did you get here? Where's your mother?"

"I came by train. Alone." She swallowed the lump in her throat.

The small oil lantern on the table by the window illuminated the side of his rugged face in dancing light. Deep lines were etched into dark skin. Though he must have been in his late fifties or sixties, his hair was still raven black. He smelled of wood smoke and stared at her as she examined his features. He shook his head and stepped back.

"Forgive me. Please come in. I just can't believe you're here."

Sasha ducked away from a moth seeking the light, and he swatted it outside. "You are Dewey Hummingbird. . .my uncle?"

Lips that didn't look as if they'd smiled much tilted upward. "I sure am. Come on in, or we'll have half the bugs in the Creek Nation in here. Not that they'd bother me, but you. . ."

Sasha tugged her satchel inside and held it in front of her. On the seat of an old chair, she noticed a copy of *Treasure Island*, and a spark of surprise flickered through her. She had trouble imagining her uncle as an educated man. In New York, Indians were always classified by words like *savage* or *primitive.* But he had written the letter to her mother. And she'd overheard a man on the train who'd said that Creek Indians were considered one of the five civilized tribes, though she wasn't sure what he meant by that.

She glanced around the small, rustic log cabin. Much of it remained hidden in the shadows, but what she saw made her shiver. What had she gotten herself into?

"I know this place isn't much. I'm actually building a bigger house, but it's not quite done yet." He stared at her. "I can't believe you're here. It's so good to finally see you. I'd almost given up hope of you ever coming here."

She smiled at the delight twinkling in his dark eyes. "It's wonderful to meet you, too."

"Here, let me have that." He took her satchel, disappeared into a dark room off to the side, and returned. "You're an answer to prayer."

Sasha blinked. "I am?" She'd never been someone's answer to prayer before—at least not that she knew of.

Her uncle smiled. "Yes'm, you sure are. I've been praying for years that Myrtle would come for a visit and bring you." His expression sobered. "Where is your mother? Is she all right?"

Sasha nodded. "Yes, she's fine—as far as I know. She's gone to England to get married."

"Married! Well, that's a good thing, I suppose. I hope she's happy."

"I'm sure she is." Sasha pressed her lips together. She didn't want to be reminded of her mother's desertion.

He hurried over to the chair and picked up his book. "Have a seat. You must be tired. How did you get here from town?"

"I walked." She dropped down in the chair, realizing just how exhausted she truly was.

"That's a fair distance on foot." He disappeared into the

dim shadows across the room and returned carrying a glass. "Want a drink? The water here is good and cold."

She nodded. He handed her a glass with a chipped top, and she gulped down the refreshing liquid.

Her uncle pulled a wooden chair away from the small table and sat across from her. His face burst into a smile again. "Thank the good Lord. I just can't believe you're really here. You look much like your mother did when she was young, Anastasia."

"Please call me Sasha. Anastasia is so formal."

He nodded. "And you may call me Dewey—or Uncle—or whatever you'd like.

Never having met anyone who'd known Cybil when she was young before, Sasha considered his comment about her looking like her mother when she was younger. There was something special about it.

"How long can you stay?"

Sasha tightened her grasp on the wooden arms of the chair, unsure how to respond. The trip to Tulsa had cost much more than she'd anticipated, and unless she found some work she could do, she was stranded.

"I. . .uh, I don't know. How long would you like me to stay?"

His gaze darted around the cabin. "This ain't what you're used to, what with your having lived in those fancy places in New York and all, but you're welcome to stay as long as you like. Or at least as long as you think you can stand it." He chuckled as if he'd made a joke.

"I would like to stay awhile and get to know you, if you're sure you don't mind."

"You're welcome to stay forever if you want." He smiled. "I'm just happy to finally get to meet you and have family here again. But you look all tuckered out. How about you get some rest, and we can talk more in the morning? Unless you'd rather have something to eat first."

"I am a bit hungry, but I don't want you to go to any trouble."

"No trouble." He stood. "You like peaches?"

Sasha nodded. "Yes, that sounds good. Thank you."

He shuffled toward her with a twig in his hand and stuck it in the lantern. It flamed to life, and he used it to light another lamp on the other side of the room. The insides of the primitive cabin shocked her. How could anyone live with so little? Two small pots hung below a wooden rack that held several plates and cups. A tiny table rested against the far wall. The mate to the chair her uncle had used looked lonely sitting there by itself.

"I don't have company too often. Just my workman. He and I take most meals together. Hey, can you cook?"

She shook her head. "Not really. I always wanted to learn, but I never got the opportunity, living in hotels most of my life."

"That's too bad. I'm not much of a cook myself."

He opened a jar of peaches, spooned out several, then handed her a bowl and sat back down in the chair. Though elderly, he seemed to get around well and was able to take care of himself.

The sweet, yet tart, juice of the peach teased her tongue, and she stuffed the slice the rest of the way in her mouth. "Mmm. . .these are delicious. New York's peaches don't taste anything like this."

"Your grandma planted our peach trees when she was young. I share the harvest with a neighbor lady, and she cans them for me."

Sasha looked up. Surprise zinged through her insides at the mention of her grandmother. "Tell me about my grandmother."

He grinned. "I can do that. Her name was Adele Humming-bird, and she was my brother's wife."

"Your brother? My grandfather?"

"James was his name. He was my older brother by four years, but he passed away several years ago. We had a much younger sister named Kizzie." He rubbed his chin and looked away for a moment. "She died last year."

A deep sense of losing something precious left Sasha weak. If she'd only known about her family sooner, she could have met her aunt. "I'm sorry."

He waved aside her concern. "Kizzie lived a good life. It's because of a promise I made her that I'm building a new house."

Sasha finished the peaches and handed the bowl to her uncle.

"I reckon we ought to get you settled for the night." He pushed up from his chair, set the bowl on the table, and returned for the lantern.

Sasha yawned, not wanting to move. She'd barely slept any the night before for fear the two men would find her. When she had fallen asleep, she'd dreamed about the handsome cowboy saving her. Finally, she forced her exhausted body up and followed her uncle into the tiny bedroom. She longed to hear more about her family, but it could wait until morning.

Her uncle set the lantern on a small table next to a single bed. On the far wall were several pegs that she imagined held all of her uncle's clothes. He grabbed a plaid shirt off one peg and a blanket that was lying over the back of the only chair in the room.

"Make yourself at home. There's an outhouse back of the cabin. . .if'n you've need of it."

Sasha was sure her uncle's cheeks had darkened a shade. Suddenly, she realized he was offering her his room. "Oh no, I can't take your bed. I don't mind sleeping on the floor. Truly."

She reached for the blanket, but he tugged it away.

"No, I'll bed down in my workman's tent with him. He won't mind at all."

"But—"

"No buts. You're my guest, and I'm happy you're here. Have a good rest. I'll see you in the morning after the cock crows."

He turned and left before she could argue. Exhausted, she untied her shoes and tossed them under the chair. She blew out the lamp and flopped on the bed, thinking about her ancestors. Her grandparents had names now—James and Adele Hummingbird.

Smiling in the dim lighting, she thought about her talkative uncle. She liked him, but she couldn't help feeling thankful that she hadn't been raised in such rugged circumstances.

But what about now? Could she handle living like he did?

The truth suddenly hit her—she truly was of Indian blood. She might never know about her father's side of the family, unless maybe Uncle Dewey knew something, but at least she now had a heritage. If only she could embrace it.

five

Sasha held her uncle's arm as they left the family grave plot where her grandparents and aunt and uncle Arbuckle were buried. It saddened her to think she had family she could have gotten to know if only her mother had brought her for a visit.

"Yes'm, Kizzie led a good life. Her only regret was not having children." He patted Sasha's hand. "She'd have loved you and mothered you half to death."

She smiled. "I would have liked that. May I ask how she died?"

"The doctor said her heart just gave out. Folks around here loved Kizzie. She was always doing something nice for someone."

Dewey led her past the cabin and up a hill. Off to her right she heard a whack, followed by a pause, and then another whack. Her uncle glanced past her as the pattern of sounds continued.

"That's my workman chopping wood. He's a fine boy. You'll like him."

Sasha wasn't so sure of that. Any boys she'd been around had always been ornery troublemakers.

"Kizzie struck oil on her land. She died a wealthy woman." Dewey shook his head. "I didn't want her money, but she left it and her land to me. Made me promise to build a nice house for myself. Said to make it big enough just on the chance you and your mother might come back some day."

Sasha turned her head and stared at him. "She actually said that?"

"Yes'm, she sure did."

With an uncommon lightheartedness warming her chest, she lifted her skirts with her free hand and allowed her uncle to propel her up the hill. As they reached the top, she gasped out loud. The rising sun, hidden directly behind the large house, made it look as if the structure had a shiny golden halo. The two-story brick home, in the final stages of completion, would rival anything in New York, but it looked so out of place here in the wilds of Indian Territory.

"It's too fancy for my blood, but I promised Kizzie—and now that you're here, I'm glad I did." Dewey glanced at her, and for the first time, he looked shy—hesitant. "You like it?"

"Oh, yes! It's lovely. Can we go in?"

"I don't see why not. The workers should be here anytime, but we'll stay out of their way.

The double doors opened into a tall foyer, which included a beautiful curved staircase. Sasha's mouth hung open, but she couldn't help it. She felt as if she'd walked into Cinderella's castle.

The scent of fresh wood tickled her nose, and her footsteps echoed in the empty structure. Elegant dark wood rose three feet from the wide baseboards and was topped by a delicate wainscoting. Above that, all the walls were plain. Her mind raced with ideas. She envisioned a lovely floral wallpaper in the foyer. . .

Some time later, they stood in the room she'd picked for her own at her uncle's request. They opened the double doors and walked out on the wide balcony overlooking a small lake. Ducks quacked to one another as they splashed in the pristine water. Far off to her right, she could see the tips of several derricks, but no other oil equipment obliterated the view.

"It's so lovely here."

Dewey moved to her side. "Yes'm, it is. I've had plenty of those oilmen out here wanting me to lease them my land for drilling, but I want to keep it the way God made it. I don't need the money, but I need for the land to stay the way it was when our people first came here."

"I'm glad you feel that way. I know oil has made many people wealthy and the country needs it, but I saw how it ruins the land."

He nodded, and they stood together in silence, enjoying the view and the cool breeze. In spite of the rustic setting, Sasha felt as if she'd finally come home. Was it possible to find her roots in this place?

"I used to farm mostly, but now I run a couple hundred head of cattle. Those oilmen like their beef." Dewey turned to face her. In the daylight his wrinkles were magnified, but his eyes reflected the kindness she heard in his voice. He was no savage, just a man with Indian heritage.

As much as she ached to belong to someone or some place, she still couldn't reconcile with the fact that she was a half-breed. She may not ever have met her father, but it was evident by her lighter skin tone that she wasn't full-blooded Creek. Would she be welcomed into the Creek Nation or considered a despised outcast?

"Did you know my father?"

Dewey shook his head. "No. You're mother must have met him after she left here." He stretched and turned to face her. "So, what do you think? Could you stay and furnish this house for me? I might know building materials, but I know nothing about home furnishings and all the fripperies a fancy house like this needs."

She shook off her disappointment that Dewey didn't know

her father and allowed excitement to soar through her at all the possibilities for the house.

"I've more money than I could spend in a lifetime, so you can do whatever suits your fancy."

A wave of apprehension washed over her. Would it be taking advantage of her uncle in some way to spend his money?

He flapped his hand in the air. "I see your mind working, missy. This is your home, too. I want you to feel you can stay as long as you like, and if you need to leave, you'll always have a place to return to. And when I'm gone, this will be yours. You and your mom are the only kin I've got left."

Unshed tears stung Sasha's eyes at her uncle's surprising kindness, and she looked at the lake so she wouldn't embarrass him. Even her own mother had never treated her as lovingly as this man she'd only met twelve hours ago.

A loud whistle broke the natural quiet, and Sasha searched for the source. She could see someone walking toward the house in the shadows of the trees, but he was too far away to tell much about him. It must be her uncle's worker.

Dewey tapped his watch. "Yep, right on time. C'mon, I want you to meet my boy. He's like a son to me."

They reached the bottom of the curved stairs just as the front door opened. Sasha sucked in a breath. The man who'd come to her rescue twice walked into the room. A good six-feet tall, he wore a blue chambray shirt and dusty jeans. This was certainly no boy, but a handsome, well-built man. Jim Conners, her champion.

Her mouth went dry as she stood on the bottom step and watched him set down his crate of tools. He removed his hat, and his thick thatch of ebony hair flopped back down, giving him a roguish air. Her heart skittered as his dark, surprised gaze landed on her. His eyes were nearly as black as her uncle's, but his skin was a healthy sun-kissed tan, lacking the red tones that Dewey's had.

"Lookee here, Jimmy boy. We've got us a guest."

✤

Jim's mouth felt dry as a desert as shock rippled through him. The last thing he expected to see in his boss's new house was a beautiful woman. As he continued to stare, her cheeks turned a dark rose, and she finally glanced away.

"Jimmy, this is my niece, Anastasia Di Carlo. She's from New York City."

Unaccustomed to being taken off guard, Jimmy struggled to gather his composure and stepped forward, hat in hand. He crinkled the brim and licked his lips, hoping to find his voice. He held out his hand. "Jim Conners. Nice to meet you, ma'am."

Her eyes sparkled, and she reached out, shaking his hand. "It's my pleasure, Mr. Conners."

Jim's gaze collided with hers. There was something familiar about her saddle brown eyes. His mouth opened, then he slammed it shut. This was the woman from the hotel! He was certain.

She cleared her throat, and Dewey chuckled. Jim realized he was staring and still held her hand. He released it as if it were a rattler and stepped back.

"She's a sight to behold, ain't she?" Dewey waggled his eyebrows.

Jim nodded, searching his mind for any conversation he'd had with Dewey about a niece. He drew a blank. All the times they'd worked together and ridden to church or town, Dewey had never mentioned having family outside of Indian Territory. In fact, as far as he knew, all of Dewey's family had already passed on. But now Dewey's niece had arrived, and

Jim had a feeling his life would never be the same.

His heart stampeded as he looked at Miss Di Carlo again. She had to be one of the most beautiful women he'd ever seen. She studied him, as he did her. She'd tied her long brown hair back with a ribbon, but rebellious waves that refused to be tamed wafted around her face. His eyes followed her narrow nose down to lips that looked soft and kissable.

He lowered his gaze to the floor. Where in the world had that thought come from?

Maybe he had romance on the brain since his sister, Katie, had recently found love and marriage.

"Sasha is gonna be in charge of decorating the house."

"Sasha?" Jim glanced at Dewey.

The older man waved his hand. "Sasha's what folks call her. You can, too."

Jim glanced at Miss Di Carlo to see if she agreed. She gave him a soft smile and gentle nod of her head, which sent his pulse racing.

Oh brother. This wasn't good. He enjoyed looking at a beautiful woman like any man, but he'd never reacted so strongly to one before. He couldn't afford to have an attraction to his boss's niece. He needed this job so he could save his money and buy land in the Oklahoma Territory near his aunt and uncle's farm.

"It's fine if you want to call me Sasha, Mr. Conners. I imagine we'll be seeing lots of each other since you work for my uncle."

"Then you must call me Jim." He swallowed, grateful that he'd finally found his voice again.

Her pretty smile sent pleasant shivers skittering through him, but he tried to ignore them. Sasha Di Carlo had a sweet, innocent look about her, but the hair on the back of his neck had stood up at the mention of her spending Dewey's money. It made sense to have a woman furnish the house, but he had heard many stories of long-lost relatives showing up when one of the families in the area struck oil. Dewey had only been granted control of Kizzie Arbuckle's money in the last six months. He hoped this woman really was Dewey's niece and not just another fortune hunter. Just maybe he should keep his eye on her.

"You gonna have breakfast with us?" Dewey hooked his thumbs through the straps of his overalls.

Jim shook his head. "I just had some jerky and bread. I wanted to see what else needs to be finished up before we let the workers go. But I think we've just about got it licked." His gaze traveled around the room. Pride for doing a job well swelled his chest. This home would be a legacy to his skills as a carpenter long after he was gone.

"Sounds good. Well, Sasha and me went for a walk before eating, and now my belly button's rubbing against my backbone. We're heading back to the cabin. Maybe at dinner tonight you and Sasha could talk about furnishing this place." He scratched his head. "I don't know what Kizzie was thinking, wanting me to build a house this big, but it's done. Guess we'll just have to let the good Lord fill it."

Jim stood at the door and watched Dewey and Sasha walk back to the cabin. Sasha glided along, her skirts skimming the tops of the wildflowers. She was a sight to behold, for sure. No woman had stirred his blood like she had in a very long time.

He thought about the aunt and uncle who'd raised him. He missed Mason, Rebekah, and their children a lot, but he missed his sister, Katie, and his nephew, Joey, the most. He was glad that Katie had found love again with the bounty hunter who'd saved her life. Dusty McIntyre was a good man and would treat her well. Much better than their own father ever had.

Jimmy remembered the last time he ever saw his father, at the sight of the first Oklahoma land rush near Guthrie. Even as a seven-year-old, he knew his pa wasn't the fatherly type. In fact, he was a gambler and a liar and had left his wife and two children alone while he sought adventure.

Thanks to Uncle Mason's patient guidance and Dewey's influence, his heart was right with God again. Jim lifted his gaze toward heaven, praising God for the beauty of the new day.

He liked to think he was honorable and kind, but he had no patience for a liar or a deceiver. He'd seen at a young age the trouble a swindler could cause. "Please, God, let Dewey's niece be the real thing and not just some treasure seeker out to get his money."

It would break his heart if Sasha hurt Dewey. He loved the old man like a father. Maybe he'd just keep an eye on Sasha Di Carlo until he was certain about her.

What could it hurt?

six

Dewey's wet shirt snapped in the air as Sasha gave it a quick shake. She pulled two clothespins from her apron pocket and secured the chambray top to the line. As she pulled a pair of socks from the wicker basket, she listened to the sounds of nature all around her. It saddened her to think of all the years that she had rarely heard birds and crickets chirping, except for when she'd ventured out to a park. The clamor of the big city had overpowered the gentle sounds of nature.

She fastened the socks to the line with wooden pins, then shook out a pair of overalls. Dewey had been both shy about her doing his laundry and delighted, telling her that all the bending aggravated the catch in his back. As she straightened a denim strap, she overheard upraised voices coming from the front of the cabin. Just as she'd come outside, she'd heard the hoofbeats of several horses coming down the dirt road, but she had continued with her task, knowing that whoever it was had not come to see her.

She pinned the overalls onto the line, picked up her basket, and walked around the side of the house.

"I've told you before, I won't have my land destroyed by oil drilling. My answer is no."

Hearing the anger in her uncle's voice, Sasha set down the basket and peered through a crape myrtle bush to see three men dressed in suits all but surrounding Dewey. She didn't want to eavesdrop but also didn't want to leave her uncle alone. Glancing over her shoulder, she considered running up the hill to find Jim but decided it would take too long.

"Surely, Mr. Hummingbird, you understand how wealthy you could be if you leased your land to Chamber Oil for drilling. All your neighbors—even your own sister—struck oil." The shortest man of the trio pushed his hat back on his head and set his hands on his hips.

"It's as close to a sure thing as you can get." A heavy-set man with a handlebar moustache held out both of his chubby hands.

Dewey shook his head. "I don't need any more money. I'm satisfied with what I have. Preserving the land and raising my cattle is what's important to me."

A tall man, who looked part Irish, stepped forward. He ran his hand over his slicked-down red hair, and his eyes gleamed as he studied her uncle. "We don't normally do this, but I have permission from the boss to make you a special offer. If you'll lease your land to Chamber Oil, we'll give you a higher royalty rate than normal, like we did with your sister. That's more than fair."

Dewey shook his fist in the air. "Fair! You call it fair when you leased Elmer Red Hawk's land for two hundred dollars an acre and yet you took out millions of dollars in oil?"

The tall man's gaze narrowed, and he stepped forward. "Mr. Red Hawk was more than pleased with the deal in the beginning, but he got greedy."

"And now he's dead." Dewey crossed his arms over his chest. The finality in his voice made Sasha shudder.

The three men closed ranks and stepped forward. "You accusing us of something, old man?" the tall man hissed.

"You'd be wise to lease us your land and stop spreading rumors."

Sasha didn't like the man's tone of voice or his threat. She grabbed Dewey's rifle, which leaned against the side of the house where he'd been cutting brush, and stepped around the bush, out into the open. Cocking a bullet into the chamber as Dewey had taught her the day before, she braced the rifle against her shoulder and glared at the trio. She may not know how to shoot yet, but with a background in theater, she sure could pretend that she did. "Is there a problem here?"

Their eyes widened at the sound of her voice, and at least one mouth dropped open. Tall Man responded first, as his face altered from surprised to sickly sweet. "Well, how do, ma'am. We didn't realize ol' Dewey had gone and gotten himself a woman." He let out a low whistle through his teeth. "Whoowee, Dewey, you ol' coot, you like 'em young."

Surprise rocked Sasha, but she quickly recovered. "I am not his woman; I'm his niece."

"That a fact? Didn't know Dewey had any kin left." The fat man smoothed his forefinger over his moustache and glanced at Tall Man.

Sasha hiked up her chin and the barrel of the heavy weapon. "Well, he does. And it's time you got off his land."

Dewey chuckled and relieved her of the rifle. "I guess you all had better listen to the lady. You've heard all I've got to say, so get out." He waved the rifle toward them, and all but the tallest man stepped back.

"I reckon we'll give you some more time to think things over, but we'll be back."

He turned and stomped toward his horse. The poor animal squealed when the man jerked hard on the reins and turned it toward town.

Sasha sighed as they rode off. It seemed to her as if the white men were the troublemakers in this part of the country rather than the Indians.

Dewey turned to face her. "Sorry you had to see that. Them fellows have been after me for nearly a year to allow them to drill on my land. I keep telling them it's not going to happen, but they don't take the hint."

"Well, maybe now that I'm here they'll leave you alone. They're less likely to bully you if there's a witness around."

Dewey smiled and hugged her shoulders. "I imagine it was the rifle what scared them off, and not you. Though I do appreciate the assistance."

Sasha sagged against him, fearing her shaky legs would give out. Those men would be back—she was almost certain of it. They had to be ready if and when that happened. But how could a woman and an old man fight off three grown men if push came to shove? Her mind started whirling. Somehow she had to help her uncle keep his land and not let those oilmen bully him into doing something he would regret. But how?

&.

"I don't reckon Keaton looks like much of a town to you after living in New York." Dewey jiggled the reins to encourage the horses pulling his wagon. "It wasn't even here back when your mother lived with us."

"It is a lot different, that's for sure." Keaton was typical of the small towns Sasha had passed through on her way here except, like Tulsa, it sported many new buildings made from fresh wood that hadn't grayed yet. A few brick or stone buildings were scattered among them.

Unlike the day she arrived last week when things were somewhat quiet, now scores of people milled around. Local oilmen had invited the townsfolk to a huge pig roast to celebrate the railroad coming to Keaton. Instead of the long wagon ride to Tulsa, now folks could get there in less than a half hour. Sasha knew trains were good news for the town, but she'd had her fill of them for a while. One good thing was that it would make retrieving her trunk easier and less time consuming. She hoped to make arrangements today to have it delivered to the Keaton depot.

Dewey pulled the wagon alongside several others and set the brake, then climbed down and lifted his hand to assist her. Once on the ground, Sasha shook out her skirts, grateful for the breeze that cooled her legs. She desperately needed her trunk and something different to wear, although she worried that her dresses would be too fancy for this small town.

She took Dewey's proffered arm and allowed him to guide her through the crowd. Poor oil workers dressed in grimy overalls, leading their barefoot children and wives, mingled with businessmen sweating in their fancy three-piece suits. Somewhere above the noise of the crowd she heard some lively music. At booths decorated with red, white, and blue sashes, craftsmen hawked their wares. The fragrant scent of pork being roasted over a fire mixed with the aromas of fresh baked bread and pastries. Sasha's mouth watered, and excitement rippled through her at the chance to sample life in Smalltown, America.

A man stared at her as she and her uncle walked toward him. He nudged another man in the side, and both raised their eyebrows and gawked at her. She averted her gaze and watched some Indian children playing stickball.

"You want to go listen to the music or look through the commodities for sale first?" Dewey glanced down at her.

Sasha shrugged. "It doesn't matter to me."

"Then let's check out the merchandise. I could use a new hat."

As they meandered through the area where various items were displayed in the backs of wagons or on blankets on the ground, Sasha's frustration grew. Everywhere she went men stared at her—young and old. She hated being the focus of their attention and had often longed for plainer features. She wished that she'd been able to wear her costume, but then Uncle Dewey didn't know about it, and she wasn't sure he'd understand why she needed it.

A nice-looking man dressed in a clean white shirt and black denim pants walked toward her, cap in hand. A shy grin twittered on his lips as he cleared his throat. "Hullo, Mr. Hummingbird." Though he acknowledged her uncle, his gaze never left Sasha's face.

"Howdy, Spencer. Nice day for a celebration."

The man nodded and fiddled with his cap. "Yes, it is."

Dewey's mouth tilted up in an ornery grin. "Have you met my niece? Sasha Di Carlo."

The man shook his head. "A pleasure, ma'am. I was. . .uh. . . wondering if you'd do me the honor of eating with me."

Oh no, not again. Sasha stifled a sigh. The man seemed nice, and she didn't want to hurt his feelings. She offered him a smile. "Thank you, Mr. uh. . ."

"Jones. Spencer Jones."

"Mr. Jones, I truly appreciate your kind invitation, but I've just arrived in town and want to spend some time with my uncle today."

Disappointment tugged at his pleasant features. "Maybe another time then."

Not wanting to encourage him, she refrained from smiling. He tipped his hat, bid them good day, and wandered off. She heaved a sigh that made Dewey chuckle.

"You might as well get used to invitations like that. There's two dozen men to every woman in these parts. And few women are as lovely as you."

"Thank you, Uncle, but I'm not interested in getting a

husband. I just want to spend time with you right now."

"Then I don't reckon you'll want to eat with him, either."
Dewey nudged his chin toward the street.

Sasha squinted and lifted her hand over her eyes. Another
tall man strode toward her. Her cheeks puffed up as she exhaled
a sigh again, but suddenly she recognized the man coming her
direction. Jim Conners.

Her heart jolted, and a butterfly war was loosed in her
stomach as she watched his easy, long-legged gait. He was a
man confident with his body but not arrogant. He lifted his
hat in greeting, and Sasha smiled. His damp black hair had
melded to his head, and a ring marked where his Western hat
had rested.

"You all been to dinner yet?" Jim's hopeful gaze darted from
Dewey to Sasha.

"Nope, not yet." Dewey's lips turned up in a wry grin, and
he glanced at her, eyebrows raised.

Jim's warm smile melted her remaining defenses, and she
gave a little nod.

"You want to join us, Jimmy?"

For some reason she welcomed Jim's attentions where she
shunned others—maybe because he'd twice come to her aid.
He held out his elbow, and she looped her arm through his,
ignoring the sparks from his touch and her uncle's soft chuckles.
She'd had plenty of handsome men escort her to events in New
York, but somehow this simple carpenter intrigued her more
than any man she'd ever known.

She peered up at him, wondering again if he maybe had
Indian blood. A trickle of sweat slipped down his temple,
and he glanced at her, locking eyes. Something sparked in his
gaze, and Sasha knew without a doubt that she wanted to get
to know this man better.

seven

What little Sasha had eaten of the roasted pork and the fresh green beans and potatoes seasoned with ham had been delicious. But with Jim Conners sitting directly across from her, making eye contact every few minutes as he and Dewey chatted, her appetite had fled.

She tried to pinpoint what it was about Jim that interested her. He was very easy on the eyes, especially when she glimpsed his quick smile. Where her uncle's teeth more resembled a picket fence, Jim's were straight and white.

Maybe she liked him because he was kind to her uncle and actually seemed interested in what he had to say. Or maybe it was the compassion he'd shown her when he gave an old woman a ride.

Sasha pressed her lips together and watched as a group of Indians in colorful native costumes danced on the vaudeville stage. She especially enjoyed the little children as they pounded out the drum's rhythm with their tiny feet. If she had been raised here, would she have learned to dance like them?

Dewey cleared his throat, and she looked at him. "I'd like to go look at them new-fangled automobiles on display."

Sasha stood and picked up her tin plate. "I'll go with you. I saw plenty of automobiles in New York—even rode in a couple—but I don't mind seeing what they have here."

Dewey glanced at Jim, who'd stood up at the same time as Sasha. "I thought Jimmy might escort you over to watch the show for a while."

Her gaze darted to Jim's and back to her uncle. Did Dewey have some business to attend to and not want her around, or was he perhaps trying to pair her off with Jim?

"You might enjoy the show. You probably haven't seen real Indian dancers before." Jim glanced at her, his hopeful gaze making her waver.

Maybe spending time with Jim was a good thing. If he escorted her, surely other men would leave her alone so she could enjoy herself. She glanced at Dewey. "Are you sure you don't mind?"

"Nah." Dewey waved his hand in the air. "You two young'uns go enjoy the show."

Sasha and Jim carried their tin plates to the wash table, then he offered his arm. She looped hers around his, marveling again at the tingles tickling her insides. He found her a seat on a rough bench and sat beside her, keeping a decent distance.

Her gaze riveted to the low stage where children were stomping around in a wide circle, while sometimes spinning around in a smaller one. Off to the side a group of older men chanted a monotone tune and pounded on drums of various sizes.

Jim leaned toward her. "That's called the stomp dance. Can't imagine where they came up with such an original name."

She glanced at him, and his black eyes twinkled with mirth. Smiling at his joke, she watched as the children finished and left the stage. A man with trained dogs followed. The lively animals did some amazing tricks. Next came an opera singer, whose shrill voice made Sasha cringe.

In spite of the woman's less-than-stellar performance, Sasha relished sitting back and being part of the audience and enjoying the show instead of having to race around applying makeup or preparing to go onstage herself.

The singer attempted a high note and missed. Beside Sasha, Jim squirmed on the bench. He leaned forward, fiddling with his hat, but she was certain he held his hands over his ears on purpose.

She pressed her lips together but couldn't help laughing. He glanced back at her, his neck reddening when he caught her watching him. Sasha leaned over, wanting to put him out of his misery. "Would you mind if we go look at some of the wares that are for sale?"

Relief brightened his countenance, and he jumped up, offering her his hand. She took it and allowed him to guide her out of the quickly dwindling crowd. She felt sorry for the performer, but not enough to endure any more of her strained singing.

Jim tucked Sasha's hand around his muscled arm again. She glanced up at him, proud to be escorted by such a nice-looking man. That she felt so comfortable with him surprised her. Still, she didn't want to get her hopes up that he might have feelings for her. They'd barely just met. He might be willing to escort her around town, but what white man would want a relationship with a half-breed?

Her uncle had told her about the Upper Creeks, who were full-blooded like him, and the Lower Creeks, who were of mixed race. Sasha felt stuck between two worlds—that of the whites and that of the Upper Creeks, which was her heritage—neither of which would completely accept a woman of mixed race.

"So, what do you want to look at?"

Jim's question pulled her from her troubled musing. She glanced around, and her gaze landed on a colorful display of handmade quilts. She pointed toward them. "There. Uncle Dewey might like a locally made quilt for his new room, rather than something fancier from a store."

Jim nodded and guided her toward a clothesline tied between two trees. Three beautiful quilts hung there, brightening the stark landscape. Sasha loosened her grip on Jim and lifted the edge of a multi-colored coverlet. Though the fabric in the design looked to be from previously worn clothing, nobody could deny the quality of the tiny stitches.

Jim leaned over her shoulder. "These are made by the oil widows."

She peered up at him, nearly gasping at his nearness. He stared at her a moment before stepping back. "Oil widows?" she finally rasped.

He nodded. "Most often when an oil worker dies, his family has so little money that they continue to live in Rag Town. Some of the widows collect used clothing and make these quilts. Nice, aren't they? I took a couple home last time I went."

Sasha longed to ask him about his home but thought it would be improper since they barely knew each other. She refocused on the quilt. "What colors do you think Uncle Dewey would like best?"

Jim moved to the quilt beside her. "Seems like most of his shirts are some shade of blue. I guess he might like this one."

Sasha studied the design that was mostly blue and white with a little red and green. A woman who'd been helping a customer sidled up beside Jim. "That's a flying geese pattern. See, it loosely resembles a flock of geese in flight."

Sasha nodded but turned her eyes toward on the woman. She couldn't be too much older than Sasha, but she had a haggard look about her. The worn dress hung on her thin frame as if she'd lost weight since making it. A towheaded boy about four years old ran toward her and hid behind the woman's skirt.

"I see you, Philip." A darling urchin with wispy blond locks skipped in their direction. She reached behind the woman and touched the boy. "Tag, you're it." The girl smiled at Sasha and darted away with the barefoot boy close on her heels.

"I'm sorry for the interruption, but children are good at that." A red blush stained the woman's pale cheeks as she studied the ground.

"It's all right. I grew up with kids all around." Jim's kind words were meant to soothe the woman, but a spear of shame pierced Sasha's heart. She'd never been wealthy, but she'd always worn pretty clothes and shoes. Never once had she been required to go barefoot or wear frayed rags like those poor children. Though she'd only planned to buy her uncle a quilt, she changed her mind and bought a second one to help out the poor widow.

Jim held her purchase while Sasha dug around in her handbag for the money Dewey had given her. She felt a bit odd spending money that wasn't hers, but she was furnishing his home as he had requested. Sasha handed the woman ten dollars, but a frantic looked passed across her face.

"I'm sorry, ma'am, but I have no change." Her gaze darted between Sasha's and the ground, as if she were afraid Sasha might change her mind about the purchase.

"I have some money." Jim stuck his hand in his pocket.

Sasha touched his arm. "That's all right. I don't need any change."

Jim's eyes sparked with surprise, but the woman took a step backward as if she'd been slapped. "Oh, no. I couldn't possibly accept more than the quoted price."

"But—" Jim's light touch on her back halted Sasha's objection. She didn't mind the woman keeping the whole ten dollars. It was obvious she needed the money.

Jim pulled out eight dollars and handed it to the lady and

gave Sasha's money back. "I'll square things with Dewey later."

As they walked away, she glanced up at Jim. "Why wouldn't she accept more than the price?"

"Stubborn pride." He pressed his lips together. "As much as she needed the money, she still wouldn't accept more than what she thought was fair. That would be charity. And she'd never accept charity."

Sasha pondered his words as she purchased a soft pair of beautifully beaded moccasins from another vendor. They would be nice to wear around the house instead of her uncomfortable shoes. She followed Jim to the wagon, where they deposited their purchases. He checked on the horses, then came around to stand next to her, leaning his elbows against the side of the wagon. She nibbled her lip, knowing she still owed him a thank you.

"I want you to know how much I appreciated your help at Whitaker's Hotel."

A charming smile tugged at his lips. "I thought that was you. I didn't get too good of a look, what with things happening so fast and all."

"Yes, well, I did scurry out of there rather quickly." Sasha returned his smile as she studied his handsome face. His hair and eyes were black as midnight. His skin, darkly tanned. He was tall like a towering pine tree, and his powerful, well-muscled body moved with an easy grace. She'd never admit to watching him work, but she enjoyed doing so. He glanced away, staring off at the crowd, and Sasha realized she'd spent too long observing him. Heat warmed her cheeks, and she searched for a safe topic.

"So, you had a bunch of siblings?"

"What?" Jim glanced at her, his brows puckered. "No, only one—a sister."

Sasha blinked. "But I thought you said you grew up around a lot of kids."

Jim chuckled. "I did. But they were my cousins, not siblings. My aunt and uncle raised me after my parents died."

A wave of guilt washed over Sasha for bringing up the subject. "I'm sorry about your parents."

"It was a long time ago." He flipped his hand in the air and pushed away from the wagon. "I guess we ought to track Dewey down and make sure he hasn't gotten into any trouble."

Sasha peeked up at Jim, unsure if he was serious or teasing. She remembered seeing the three men who'd accosted Dewey and wished now that they'd all stayed together. She'd just found her uncle and didn't want anything to happen to him.

"My family lives in the Oklahoma Territory," Jim said, as he guided her back toward the throng of people. "Uncle Mason has a farm there. Ever been on a farm?"

She shook her head, wondering what it would be like to live away from a big city most of your life. Allowing Jim to lead her, she marveled at how comfortable he was to be with and to talk to. It was almost as if they were friends.

Suddenly, Jim stopped, and she stumbled to a halt. "Not again." A muscle ticked in his jaw and his gaze narrowed.

Sasha looked around, trying to figure out what had raised his ire, and she saw her uncle surrounded by the same three men who had visited the ranch the day before. Jim tugged her out of the main flow of people and tucked her up against the millinery store. "Stay here."

Because of the noise of the crowd, she couldn't make out Dewey's conversation, but she did hear "cheat Indians" and "can't read" when he lifted his voice. She edged around some old men sitting in front of the barbershop, hoping to get close enough to hear.

Jim marched up to the trio and shoved his hands to his hips. Dewey glanced at him, looking a bit relieved. "You men are slow learners. Mr. Hummingbird is not interested in leasing his land."

"He's a slow learner." Tall Man waved his hands in the air as he argued with Jim. "He could make hundreds of thousands of dollars from oil rights."

"You're just going to have to take no for an answer." Jim leaned toward the man. "Dewey's answer is no."

Tall Man's nostrils flared, and he clenched his fists. He was a good two inches taller than Jim but not nearly as well built. "You need to learn when to butt out, kid. This isn't your concern." He shoved Jim.

Taken off guard, Jim stumbled back into a picket fence. It leaned sideways from his weight but didn't break. He regained his footing and tightened his fist.

"There's no call to get rough." Dewey stepped forward holding out his hand, palms up. "We can handle this peacefully."

A man hurried past Sasha, then stopped and turn around, staring at her. A slow smile lifted his lips. "Well, hello there." He tipped his hat, and his dark eyes glimmered. "Pardon me, miss."

The well-dressed, darkly handsome man was obviously Indian. He stepped in front of Jim, virtually ignoring him. With a wave of his hand, the three men backed off and stood to the side, glowering at Jim, who glared back.

The man held out his hand to her uncle. "I'm Roman Loftus. Sorry if these men have been harassing you, Mr. Hummingbird. They tend to get a little overexcited when they smell a sure thing."

Jim relaxed his stance a bit, as did Dewey. Mr. Loftus kept his back to her, but he turned his head, displaying his perfect profile, and waved away the three men. They scowled and grumbled but walked off.

A group of men behind her laughed, and she missed hearing what Mr. Loftus said. He turned, along with Dewey and Jim, looking her way. The man's wide smile didn't warm her as Jim's did, but there was no denying his handsome looks.

She walked over to the group, and the man tipped his hat again. "Roman Loftus. It's a pleasure to make your acquaintance, Miss Di Carlo."

Sasha noticed that he already knew her name. Confidence practically oozed from him. She smiled, accepting his outstretched hand, and he grasped her fingertips, then leaned over and kissed her knuckles.

Surprised, she darted a glance at Jim. He didn't appear too happy.

Dewey nudged his head toward the man. "His father is Gerald Loftus, a prominent Creek oilman."

Surprise surged through her. She hadn't realized that some of the oil companies were actually owned by Indians rather than white men.

"Miss, it would be my great pleasure to escort you and your uncle to supper this evening."

Sasha stifled her desire to roll her eyes at his flowery actions, but the fact that he omitted inviting Jim irritated her. She glanced at her uncle, and he shrugged. She couldn't help looking at Jim, who stood frowning with his hands on his hips.

"Thank you for your kind offer, Mr. Loftus, but we ate not too long ago, and I do believe we are heading home soon, so as to make it before dark."

Mr. Loftus pressed his lips together and narrowed his eyes for such a brief moment that she wasn't sure of his intentions.

He didn't look like a man who took rejection well.

"Perhaps another time then." He smiled, tipped his hat, and strode off without a comment to Dewey or Jim.

"Arrogant—" Jim glanced at Sasha and closed his mouth.

There was very little conversation as Sasha, Dewey, and Jim gathered their purchases and readied to leave. The confrontation had broken the wonderful mood of the day.

As they headed home, Sasha peeked at Jim riding his horse beside the wagon. He looked so comfortable in the saddle. He turned his head and caught her staring. A slow smile tilted his finely shaped lips.

She looked away, hoping her time in Indian Territory would be a long one. Just maybe there was hope for a half-breed and a carpenter.

eight

Sasha studied the two carpets at the Tulsa store. One would go well with the quilt she'd purchase for her uncle, but he told her not to do anything fancy for his new bedroom. Finally, she pointed to the one with the rose design, which would go in her room. "I'll take this one. And I'd like to order some curtains out of that sheer fabric with the rose pattern we looked at earlier.

"Do you have the window measurements?" The store clerk peered up at Sasha over the top of her wire-frame glasses.

Sasha looked at Jim. He pushed away from the window he'd been staring out and reached into his pocket, withdrawing a piece of paper. He handed it to the woman, his eyes glazed with boredom. Sasha pressed her lips together to keep from smiling. Shopping obviously wasn't his favorite chore.

"I imagine you'll be needing some blinds for the windows also." The clerk glanced up from the paper expectantly. No doubt she'd make a hefty commission off Sasha's purchases.

"Yes, I will. For all the bedrooms."

A spark glimmered in the clerk's eyes, but Jim scowled. Apprehension knotted her stomach. Was he tired of waiting on her? Or did he think she was spending too much of her uncle's money?

Dewey had been adamant that money was no object. She was to furnish his home in any manner she saw fit. Still, as much fun as it was to buy furnishings, she couldn't shake feeling guilty for spending so much.

Having to pay her own way at such a young age had forced her to save her money. Spending so freely now went against every fiber of her being.

Jim stood in front of the window, again staring out. He rolled his head to the side and back as if working out the kinks. She'd tried to get him to leave her to shop when they'd first entered Mayo's Carpet store, but he'd refused. Maybe she should try again, because he was making her anxious.

"Jim."

He spun around, hope brightening his onyx eyes. "Ready to go?"

She shook her head, and his expression dimmed. "No, and it may take a while. The house has a number of windows."

"You don't have to buy everything in one day, you know." A shadow of annoyance crossed his face.

"No, but then we'd have to come to Tulsa another time. I don't want to keep taking you away from your work."

He nodded and turned toward the window again.

"I don't suppose you could go to the hardware store and see about ordering the items we need for the bathroom? That would save us some time."

Jim glanced over his shoulder, looking pleased. "I can do that. Just tell me what you want."

She explained what she and Dewey had decided, and Jim eagerly strode for the door. He stopped with his hand on the knob. "Stay here until I come back."

Sasha nodded, not sure whether to be thrilled about his protectiveness or perturbed by his bossiness.

"That husband of yours doesn't want to let you out of his sight." The clerk pushed her glasses up her nose. "He must love you an awful lot."

Sasha blinked, completely taken off guard. She wanted to

explain Jim wasn't her husband but didn't want to embarrass the kind clerk. Still, she couldn't help feeling a measure of delight being paired with such a thoughtful, pleasant-looking man.

That afternoon, Jim escorted her to her seat on the train, then went to see about getting their purchases loaded. She thumbed through one of the store catalogs, wondering what type of furniture her uncle would like for the downstairs area.

She'd been able to order some bedroom furniture and a dining set at Harper's Furniture Store but held off buying for the parlor area, hoping to get Dewey to help her. It was his home, after all.

Sasha gazed around the train. This car had seats that all faced the same direction. She let out a sigh, thankful she didn't have to sit across from any gentlemen seeking her attention. Jim slid in beside her, and her heart skipped a beat. A manly scent of sweat and dust drifted her way.

"All set." He shot a sideways glance at her. "The depot clerk said he can ship the furniture as soon as Harper's has it ready. Then we'll just have to pick it up at the Keaton depot."

"That sure makes things easier on you, doesn't it?"

He nodded and glanced at the open catalog on her lap. "More shopping?"

"Well, there's still the rest of the downstairs to furnish."

Jim pressed his lips together and turned to look out the window across the aisle. She couldn't help feeling again as if he were displeased with her for some reason. Maybe he just didn't like spending time in town.

At least she'd had a wonderful time. She thought about her afternoon with Jim. Other than showing a little impatience, he'd been a perfect gentleman all day. She loved that he was relaxed around her and not trying to win her favor. But then, he probably had no interest in a half-breed like her.

Tired, she laid her head against the window and looked out at the people scurrying around the depot. A fancy touring car pulled up and parked near the gate, and a man wearing goggles and a long travel coat hopped out and helped a woman exit the vehicle. Sasha wondered how they could stand to wear a coat in this heat.

The view triggered her memory, and she remembered the few times she had been privileged to ride in an automobile. Other than riding on a train, it had been the fastest she'd ever traveled and had nearly taken her breath away.

"Did you go to church back in New York?" Jim surprised her with his sudden question.

She shook her head. "Not too often. Mother rarely woke up before noon, and I didn't like to go alone."

Jim's eyes widened. "Noon! I never heard of people sleeping that late unless they were sick."

She couldn't help smiling at his bewildered expression. He was a man used to a full day's hard work. Seeing how antsy he was today during his idleness proved that.

"I don't know if Uncle Dewey told your or not, but Mother and I worked in the theater. She is—was—an actress, and I was a makeup artist. Mother often went out with her fans and other members of the crew after performances."

"I never knew anyone in the theater before." He grinned. "I still don't see how your ma could sleep till noon, though." He shook his head. "Anyway, I don't know if Dewey told you yet, but we generally ride together to church on Sundays, though he didn't go last week since you'd just arrived and were tired from your travels. We could take the buggy this week so you can go. That is if you want to." He stared at her as if measuring her worth.

She hadn't considered attending church but thought she

might like it and nodded. Jim smiled and leaned back, then tilted his hat so that it covered the top half of his face. His pose looked so manly it made her insides quiver.

During their evening devotions together, she had listened as Jim and Dewey talked about the different Bible verses they'd read. She'd never heard anyone talk about God as if He were a friend, and she longed to know if such a thing were possible. Though she was happier here in Indian Territory than she could ever remember, she still felt a void in her life.

Was that emptiness something a husband could fill? Or would it take Someone bigger—like God?

❧

Jim allowed the gentle rocking of the train to lull him into a relaxed stupor. Though tired from standing around shopping all day, he wasn't sleepy. Other than being half bored, he'd enjoyed his time with Sasha and felt proud walking around town with such a beauty on his arm.

Plenty of other men had noticed, and he'd stared them down, almost daring them to approach Sasha. His jaws puffed out as he sighed, knowing his behavior wasn't very Christlike. Gazing at the inside of his hat, which covered his face, he asked God's forgiveness for being boastful in his actions.

He thought of the excitement twinkling in Sasha's brown eyes and remembered her smiles and how she'd flitted from one item to the next, reminding him of a hummingbird. She had a good time today, he could tell.

But she'd spent a whole lot of Dewey's money. And enjoyed it. As much as he liked her and was attracted to her, he still wasn't sure whether to trust her.

Her timing was almost impeccable, arriving a few months after Dewey was awarded control of Kizzie Arbuckle's property and finances.

Still, he'd watched what she bought, though he doubted she realized that. She never once purchased the most expensive item. Instead, she'd leaned toward midlevel, yet quality items. He had to admit, she'd made wise purchases—practical versus showy—all except for that flowery rug she bought for her own room. Not that it was all that expensive, just too feminine for his taste.

Unable to sleep with Sasha on his mind, he pushed up and set his hat back on his head. She glanced at him, and he took a moment to study her lovely face. Delicate features highlighted an oval face. Her medium brown complexion looked as soft as a horse's muzzle. And those lips—perfect for kissing.

Her cheeks grew rosy, and she looked away. He shouldn't be staring. It might give her the wrong idea, but she was so beautiful that he was compelled to gaze on her face whenever he had opportunity. God sure did put some fine creatures on this earth.

He shook his head. What he needed to do was share the gospel with her. Obviously she'd never had any Bible training. Though she seemed to listen intently when he and Dewey talked scriptures in the evenings, she rarely asked any questions.

Maybe it was just too soon. She'd only been here a week.

Jim leaned backed and looked out the window across the aisle. The landscape sped by.

Lord, I pray You give me the opportunity to tell Sasha about You. Perhaps that's the whole reason our paths crossed. You know I haven't always walked Your path, but I am now. Help me to guide this lost lamb into the fold.

nine

Dressed in her old woman's costume, Sasha peeked out the door of the cabin, hoping Jim and Dewey were up at the new house as they'd told her they would be. Relieved not to see them, she scurried out the door and over to the buggy her uncle had hitched for her. He hadn't liked the idea of her going to town alone but thought she'd be all right as long as she was home well before dark and stayed in the good part of town.

She made a kissing smack and jiggled the reins, guiding the horse down the dirt road. Her hands trembled, and she tried to remember everything Dewey had taught her about driving a buggy. Knowing she had a mission she wanted to complete, she'd paid close attention to his instruction and now felt semiconfident of her skills.

As the horse clip-clopped down the dirt road beneath a shadowy canopy of oak, pine, and elm trees, she thought about the things Jim had told her about God the day they went to Tulsa. He'd said that the Lord was a loving God. He was alive and wanted to come into her heart. That He sent His Son Jesus to die on the cross to pay her debt of sin. It had made her heart ache to think of an innocent man dying for something she'd done.

Some of the things she'd read in the Bible made better sense now that Jim had explained them to her. She wanted the closeness with God that her uncle and Jim had, but she wasn't sure how to get it. Just asking for God's forgiveness as Jim told her to do seemed too simple. There had to be more.

As she steered the horse to the right at a fork in the road, her thoughts turned to the oil widows again. They kept invading her mind, and she remembered that cute barefoot girl dressed in rags. Jim had said the widows continued living in Rag Town because they couldn't afford to go anywhere else and that they sometimes cooked or did laundry for the oil field workers, not that it brought in much income.

The beautiful quilts and braided rag rugs the women had made would bring high prices back East. Just the fact that they were made in Indian Territory would intrigue city folk. There had to be something she could do. As the niece of a wealthy man, she doubted the widows would let her help them—but as an old Gypsy woman. . .well, perhaps.

As she neared Keaton, she drove the buggy around to the far side of town, so if people saw her, they wouldn't know she'd come from Dewey's land. On the edge of town, she parked the buggy and tied the horse to a tree. The bay gelding would be fine since her mission wouldn't take long.

Using a knobby branch for a cane, she shuffled toward the alley behind a row of fancy homes, wishing she hadn't left behind her nice cane in the scuffle at Whitaker's Hotel. Dewey had mentioned one night that some of the woman who'd gotten rich from oil threw away perfectly good clothing. They wore an item once or twice, then bought something new. He said he couldn't tolerate such waste and was perfectly happy with his worn overalls.

Sasha smiled at the memory. She doubted her uncle's overalls could take many more scrubbings on the washboard. They were nearly as ragged as the urchins' clothing.

Holding her scarf with her free hand, she worked her way down the alley. When she noticed the shimmer of bright blue fabric near a trash barrel, excitement whizzed through her. Seeing nobody around, she quickened her steps. The blue dress had been stuffed into a wooden crate. Sasha tugged it out, and a flash of lavender caught her eyes. She shook out the colonial blue skirt, trying to imagine anyone wearing something so bright. Below it lay a nearly new lavender plaid dress with leg-o'-mutton sleeves. Near the bottom of the crate lay a white eyelet blouse with a tiny stain.

She lifted out the final item and gasped out loud at the pristine white Edwardian lawn and lace tea dress. Why would anyone throw away such a beautiful garment?

After carefully folding the items, she looked around to make sure she was alone, then hoisted up the crate and hurried back to the buggy.

An hour later, in a different alley, she found several more items, but caught up in the fun of the search, she wasn't ready to quit. She glanced at the sun, knowing she still had plenty of time before she needed to start home.

Up ahead, she spotted what looked like a dark green sleeve flapping in the warm afternoon breeze behind a solid brick home. She ambled over and discovered a tea gown with a pigeon bust and lavish skirt. The dark green color would look beautiful in a quilt.

She reached for a bluish-gray item, which turned out to be a girl's pleated dress. It reminded her of the school uniform she'd worn as a child. Allowing a smile, she caressed the slightly worn garment. Maybe the little blond urchin could wear this with some minor adjustments.

Sasha couldn't believe her good fortune. She hadn't truly believed Dewey when he told her about the clothing, but she wouldn't doubt him again. She gathered up the two dresses and looked across the street. So far, she hadn't run into anyone, but she didn't want to push her luck. Could she perhaps get arrested for taking people's throw-away items? She hadn't considered that before.

She heard a door slam and some men's laughter coming from the house in front of her. She was only about twenty feet away and noticed that a window near the back porch was open. Something sounded like the squeal of a chair being pulled out, and the soft rumble of men's voices grew louder.

She ducked behind a huge oak that shaded the small back-yard as the voices grew clearer. Obviously the men had come into the room where the open window was. Peeking around the tree, she saw a man sitting sideways on the window sill.

"I told you it was easy, didn't I?"

She could make out several voices but couldn't see anybody except the one man.

"Yes, you did, but I have to say I didn't believe it would be so easy to cheat those Indians."

Sasha gasped. Cheat Indians? She glanced around for some place else to hide but saw nothing big enough. She pressed down the dresses so that they didn't show around the wide trunk.

A man's boisterous laugh pierced the air. "If those dumb Creeks had bothered to learn to read English, they'd know before they signed that Chamber Oil leases are written so that landowners only get a fraction in royalties of the income from the oil."

A mumble of agreements flittered around the room, and she heard what sounded like someone tapping a fork against a glass.

"Here's to getting rich."

Sasha gritted her teeth in anger as glasses clinked together. These men were deliberately cheating the Indians. She had to find out who they were so she could report them.

A narrow street passed along the right side of the home, but it would be too dangerous to attempt to go that way. The men might see her and know she'd overheard them. No, it would be far better to go down the alley and circle around. She could cross the street and wait until the men came out the front of the house, and they'd never be the wiser.

Excited that her plan was a good one, she carefully folded the two dresses and turned to hurry back to the buggy. Her heart pounded a ferocious rhythm as she stepped away from the tree. *Please don't notice me.*

She took a step. Her foot snagged on something, and she fell forward. Her right hand darted out as she tried to grab the trash barrel to keep from falling. The rickety metal container tilted her way and clanged to the ground as the pile of dresses broke her fall, making her landing painless. Holding her breath, she glanced at the window as the barrel clattered against some rocks. A man poked his head out the window.

"Hey! Someone's out back."

Sasha had heard enough. She had to get away. Pushing herself off the ground, she reluctantly left the dresses behind and hurried down the street. Everything in her wanted to break into a run, but she tried to remain calm. If she could get past the next house, she could duck between them and cross to Main Street.

Behind her she heard what sounded like a door being thrown open and slamming against the house.

"There!" someone shouted.

"Get her."

Sasha lifted up her skirts and rushed forward, but her legs weren't fast enough.

"You, there. Stop!"

Running for her life, she cut across the corner of a yard, hoping to get away. Suddenly, a large hand latched onto her shoulder, and she felt herself being hauled backward. She twisted and kicked as visions of her previous assault swarmed her memory. A second man charged forward and grabbed her arm.

Panting and with her heart racing, she gazed up at the sky. *Please God, if You're really up there, help me.*

* * *

Jim reined his horse away from crowded Main Street and down an alley. He patted his pocket, making sure he still had his package. His goal today had been to finish painting the parlor with Dewey's help, but the handle on his paintbrush had broken, thus he'd made an unscheduled trip to town.

His mind drifted to Sasha, and he smiled. She was so lovely and innocent, and as they were getting to know each other better, she was opening up and sharing more of herself. Her intelligent questions about the Bible had challenged him and Dewey. If she kept seeking God, she'd soon find Him. And that would be a happy day.

The horse jerked his head and sidestepped, making Jim look up. Several houses ahead, three people scuffled in the alley. He started to rein his horse down a different street, but his heart jolted when he realized two men were accosting a woman—the Gypsy woman!

She pushed and shoved but couldn't get free of her captors. Jim kicked his horse and charged ahead, knowing he had to help.

One man looked up. His eyes widened at Jim's approach. He released the woman and ran toward Jim. Hunkering down over his horse's neck, Jim charged his mount into the man, sending the attacker flying. The other man let go of the Gypsy and lunged at Jim. The second man climbed to his feet and ran to his friend's aid.

The old woman hurried down the alley and disappeared around the corner. Jim heard a shout and saw another man running his way. One man jerked his foot from the stirrup as the other yanked on his sleeve. The horse whinnied and jumped, as rough hands pulled Jim out of the saddle.

ten

Hidden in the shadows of Uncle Dewey's small barn, Sasha quickly removed her costume and slipped on the cotton dress she'd hidden earlier. Even with it being the button-up-the-front style like most of the women in the area wore, she could barely get it fastened because of her trembling hands.

What a close call that had been!

If not for some man riding to her aid, who knows what would have happened. She folded up her costume and put it in the hiding place, washed off her makeup, then unhitched the horse from the buggy. Standing by the pasture fence, she watched the gelding trot over to the pond and lower its big head to the water. She felt proud that she'd learned to handle a horse and buggy, thus gaining some independence.

But that independence had caused her to get hurt. Sasha leaned against the fence post and rubbed her bruised arm where one of the men had grabbed her. Both legs still felt as limp as spaghetti, but her mission had been a success, if only she hadn't lost those two dresses. At last count she'd collected six dresses, three skirts, four blouses, and a nightgown. Surely they would be a big help to the widows.

Glancing up at the lowering sun, she realized Dewey and Jim would be home soon. She needed to check on the stew her uncle had left simmering on the back of the stove and slice up some bread and tomatoes.

Turning toward the cabin, she wondered what to do with the information she'd overheard. She hated to get her uncle involved any more than he already was. Maybe Jim would know what to do. Or maybe that nice man who'd come to her uncle's aid and asked her to dinner could help. He seemed kind and treated her uncle with respect. What was his name? Ro—Roman something.

She grabbed the bucket inside the cabin door and headed to the creek for some fresh water.

"I can do that."

Sasha jumped. She'd been so deep in thought she hadn't heard her uncle's approach.

Dewey grinned. "You'd think you were expecting an Indian attack."

She handed the bucket to her uncle but couldn't resist giving him a hug. "No, not an attack, but it wouldn't surprise me if one asked me to dinner."

Dewey chuckled. "Guess that happens to you a lot, huh?"

"Too much."

"It's to be expected. You're a beautiful woman, and there are many more males around these parts than females."

"I understand that, but I don't have to like it."

Dewey headed toward the creek, chuckling. Sasha sliced a half dozen pieces of bread and cut up two large tomatoes, enjoying the simple domestic activities. After stirring the stew, she set the table, wondering why Jim hadn't returned. He and Dewey usually came back from the big house together.

Her mind drifted to thoughts of the house. Furniture should be arriving any day, and they could start decorating. Excitement made her hands tingle. It would be so much fun furnishing a whole house.

A scuffle outside pulled her from her thoughts.

"Sasha! Come quick."

Dewey's frantic voice set her feet in motion. At first all she noticed was Jim's saddled horse, but as the animal trotted toward the barn, she saw her uncle kneeling in the dirt. Her heart jumped as she saw Jim's battered body lying on the ground.

She rushed to his side, wondering what had happened. One eye was blackened, and his bloody lips were swollen twice their normal size. A goose egg with an inch-long gash had risen on his forehead.

"Oh! What do we do?" She looked to her uncle for guidance.

"Let's get him inside."

Dewey took Jim's shoulders, and she lifted his ankles. His dead weight was much greater than she'd expected. Finally, with both of them heaving and straining, they got Jim onto her bed.

"I'll get some more water. There are some rags in a box near the stove."

Sasha smoothed back Jim's dark hair. She hated seeing him so battered and hurting. Her emotions overcame her normal reserve, and she leaned over, placing a soft kiss on his cheek. Her feelings for him had grown and blossomed more than she realized. Everything in her wanted to pound whoever had done this to him.

He was such a nice man. He'd never once treated her with disrespect or acted like her being a half-breed mattered in any way.

She admired his fine dark looks and the lithe way he moved, like a man confident with his body and skills. He was always patient with her many questions about the Bible and answered her intelligently, not patronizingly, as one would answer a child. Seeing him each day made her heart soar. And when their gazes collided—oh my!

Could this be love?

Jim moved one of his legs and emitted a low groan. He murmured something unintelligible, and then the words "Gypsy woman."

Sasha stepped back with her hands on her cheeks, taking in his bloodied blue shirt. It was the same shirt her rescuer had been wearing.

This was her fault! Once again Jim had come to her aid, but this time, he'd paid a terrible price.

She ran into the kitchen and grabbed the rags, then hurried back to his side. Jim's eyes were open as she stepped back into the bedroom. He grabbed hold of her hand.

"The woman. Did she. . .get away?"

Sasha leaned closer, hoping her assumption was wrong. "What woman?"

Jim licked his puffy lips and winced. "The old Gypsy."

Sasha laid her hand on his chest. "Why would you help an old Gypsy woman?"

"God loves everyone. . .even poor. . .old women. How could I not help?"

Tears stung Sasha's eyes. She couldn't stand the thought that this kind man had been injured because of her.

Dewey hobbled in with another bucket of water. Sasha dipped a tin mug in it and helped Jim drink. He guzzled down the whole cupful, then collapsed against the bed. As she dabbed at his cuts, Sasha hoped that facial wounds were the only injuries he'd received.

"Why would someone do this to him? Jimmy never hurt a soul." Dewey glanced across the bed, his dark eyes looking pained.

"He was helping an old Gypsy that some men were accosting."

Dewey harrumphed. "Sound likes something he'd do. I

just hate to see him hurting."

"Me, too." Sasha applied some salve Dewey gave her and bandaged Jim's head. He'd remained silent as she tended him, only grimacing a time or two.

Guilt flooded her. Should she confess she was the one he aided to put his mind at ease? But how would she explain wearing her costume so he would understand?

She desperately wanted to tell him but feared the disgust she'd see in his eyes. No, she couldn't tell him. Soon, but not until he was better.

❧

Sasha's pounding heart matched the quick hoofbeats of the gelding pulling the buggy.

It had taken Jim three days to recover before he was able to work at the big house again. And even then, he only worked a few hours before coming back to his tent to rest awhile. He'd suffered no broken bones, but his ribs were bruised and his muscles sore.

It pained her to see his handsome face darkened with purple bruises and to watch him being careful with his movements.

If he knew what she planned to do today, he would have insisted on escorting her—and she couldn't have that.

To make things easier, she'd donned her Gypsy outfit, then shrugged her dress over it. A few miles from the cabin, she'd slipped off the dress and applied her makeup. Now, as she guided the buggy into Rag Town, she began to have second thoughts.

The massive tent city sprawled out in all directions. Children sat playing in the dirt or running around. Tired-looking women stood talking in small groups, hanging laundry or cooking at campfires. As far as she could see, not a man was in sight. Most likely the ones who lived here were at work in the oil fields.

Like oil spewing from a gusher, guilt washed over her. She'd never seen such poverty before. New York had its underprivileged areas, but her mother had never allowed her to travel in that part of the city or see where the impoverished lived. How did people survive in such squalor?

Here she'd been gallivanting to Tulsa and back, buying furniture and spending her uncle's money supplying his new house, while these people struggled to put food on their plates. Why did life have to be so lopsided?

Curious stares surveyed her as she drove through the shantytown. She tried to decipher what else she read in the tenants' eyes and decided it must be hopelessness. She knew a bit about that. Hadn't she felt hopeless of ever earning her mother's love? And in the end, she'd failed.

A swath of color grabbed her attention, and Sasha recognized the quilt hanging on the line to be of the same pattern as the one she'd bought Uncle Dewey. A woman in a baggy gray cotton dress stepped out from behind the quilt, and Sasha knew she'd found the woman she was searching for.

Sasha clambered out of the wagon and used her stick to shuffle over to the woman. The lady approached, curiosity dancing in her blue eyes. Sasha hoped and prayed her makeup would hold up to close scrutiny, but she'd do her best not to get too near the woman.

She took a deep breath, then plodded forward, hoping her plan worked. "That fancy bed cover of yours caught my eye at the festival last week."

The woman offered a shy smile. "I didn't see you there, but it was very crowded. My name's Mary McMurphey."

Ack! Sasha hadn't considered having to give her name. She didn't want to lie, but she needed to protect her true identity. "Monique," she said, thinking her middle name sounded a bit like a Gypsy.

"Pleased to meet you." Apprehension battled curiosity in Mary's eyes.

Sasha ambled toward the crate full of dresses in the back of the buggy. "I. . .uh. . .sometimes pick through people's trash before they burn it. Found a few jewels I thought you might could use." She hoped her accent resembled a Gypsy's.

"Me? Why would you bring me anything? We've never met before."

Sasha picked up the dark blue dress and fingered the fine fabric. Mary's gaze darted from the fabric to Sasha and back. Her interest was obvious.

"I can't sew—other than to do some mending. I saw your fine quilts the other day and thought you could use these clothes to make some more."

"Oh. . .I don't know." Mary's suspicious gaze traveled past Sasha, and her eyes widened.

Sasha turned back to the buggy, lifted a dark rose-colored dress out of the back, and shook it open.

"Oh, that's so lovely. I rarely get fabric that color."

Sasha smiled to herself. "It would be a shame to just return it to a trash barrel so somebody could burn it up, but I have no use for it."

Mary licked her lips. "Well. . ..if you're sure."

Sasha nodded and laid the dress in the crate. She started to lift it before Mary changed her mind.

"Here, let me get that." Mary hoisted the crate and carried it into her tent.

Sasha prepared to mount the buggy, but Mary halted her with a hand on her shoulder. "Please, you must stay and have tea with me. I have to tell you, I prayed for more fabric, and God sent you. You're an answer to prayer."

eleven

Sasha drove the buggy back home, thinking about her time with Mary. That was the second time someone had said she was an answer to prayer. Was that possible? Could God use someone and that person not even be aware of it?

She shook the reins, urging the horse up the hill. The buggy creaked as it dipped into one rut in the road after another. These country roads were just as rugged as the landscape. She passed field after field littered with oil wells and tanks. Where the derricks stood like angry sentinels, rarely was there a tree or bush. Even the ground was blackened from oil spills. Now she understood why Dewey was so determined to keep his land undefiled.

Sasha breathed a sigh of relief as she entered Dewey's property. Here, knee-high grass and wildflowers wafted in the wind and birds chirped lively tunes. Cattle grazed peacefully on the green hills. The countryside was alive and made her feel cheerful. She'd done a good thing today.

But it hardly seemed enough. Still, she had to be careful not to steal Mary's dignity by helping her too much or too often. An occasional trip now and then should suffice. If only there were more she could do.

The wagon hit a big rut, and Sasha braced herself with her foot. She clucked to the horse as she'd seen Jim do, and the animal heaved forward, pulling her back onto level ground.

The tea Mary had offered her had been weak and sugarless, but the company was cordial, and in the muted lighting of the tent, Sasha's makeup had passed the test. It was evident that Mary held beliefs of faith similar to those of Jim and Dewey. Sasha was beginning to feel left out.

But her mother and their New York friends had rarely gone to church, except on Christmas and sometimes Easter, and they had done all right. Hadn't they?

The theater troupe had worked hard to put on superb productions. They performed in the evenings, then ate dinner afterward and spent time on the town. Sasha had usually preferred to retire to her room after dining to read before going to bed. But what had been the purpose of that life? To entertain others?

Was that a noble cause?

Never once in her life had she done anything that had given her the satisfaction she had received from taking clothes to Mary. She could still see Mary caressing the fabric, looking as if she could hardly wait until Sasha left so she could get to work.

She smiled. Yes, she'd done something good today. Her uncle would be proud, but her mother would have said Sasha had wasted her time and the fine clothing, having given it to someone who couldn't appreciate its quality.

Sighing, she thought again about her uncle's faith and Jim's. Both men were the real deal. They weren't living their lives trying to impress the wealthy people of the world. They cared for others, but more important, they cared about God.

A deep longing coursed through her. She wanted to believe like they did. Believe in a God who loved her no matter if she sometimes messed up. She glanced at the sky, wondering how one went about approaching God. Jim had said you just had to believe in Jesus and confess your sins to Him, but that still seemed too easy. Surely you had to do penance—or something.

Up ahead she saw a corner of the cabin come into view and heard the rhythmic whacking of someone chopping wood. Perhaps it was Jim, though he shouldn't be exerting himself yet. Excitement at the thought of seeing him again made her limbs weak. Suddenly, she remembered her costume, and her heart nearly jumped clear out of her chest.

Using all the muscles she had, she forced the horse to stop on the road. The stubborn animal that longed to be back home where it would be freed from its binding and fed was less than cooperative. Sasha set the brake. She grabbed her dress from under the seat, climbed down from the wagon, and darted into the woods before someone could see her.

Hiking her skirts, she hurried through the thick brush toward the creek. How could she have been so carelessly caught up in her thoughts?

Behind her she could hear the horse whinnying and pawing the dirt. Surely Jim or her uncle would come to investigate.

At the creek, she flopped down on the ground and scrubbed her face with the small jar of cold cream she kept in her pocket. She scooped up some water and splashed it on her face again and again, all the while her hands shook and heart pounded.

Jim was supposed to be working up at the house. Perhaps her uncle was the one chopping wood. She would have to be more careful in the future if she donned her costume. Using her scarf for a towel, she wiped her face. Quickly, she removed her skirt and blouse and pulled the wrinkled calico over her head. She stuffed her costume under a bush and noted the surroundings so she could find it later.

Making her way back to the wagon, she gathered a handful of wildflowers for the table. As she stepped out of the trees, she saw Jim holding on to the horse and looking around. Relief filled his eyes as his gaze landed on her.

"What are you doing?"

Her mind raced. Not wanting to lie to him, she held up her hand and showed him the bouquet. "I thought some flowers would look nice on the table."

Jim's brows dipped, and a muscle in his jaw ticked. "In these parts, we tend to our animals first, then do things like. . .uh. . . pick flowers."

Sasha ducked her head, knowing he was right. But she couldn't very well explain her frantic rush into the woods. "Sorry. I'll do better next time."

"That's all right. You're new to the area." He released the brake, and the horse started of its own accord. The wheels on the buggy squealed as it rolled forward, and Jim followed it into the barn.

With her heart still throbbing, she walked toward the cabin, disappointed at Jim's reprimand. In her heart, she wanted to please him because she liked him and was grateful for all he'd done for her.

Soon, his shadow darkened the open cabin door. Droplets of water still clung to his dark stubble from his washing off. Sasha busied herself, peeling potatoes for supper.

"Got any coffee left?"

She looked up, and their gazes collided. His black eyes glimmered, and his damp, messed-up hair gave him a cute, boyish look.

"Pretty," he said, never breaking eye contact.

Sasha's heart, which had just slowed to normal, skittered out of control again. Was he talking about the flowers in the cup on the table? Or about her?

❧

"So, what do you think? Light blue or floral wallpaper?" Sasha looked at Jim, hoping he'd help her decide which paper looked best for the foyer.

Jim glanced at the paper, then at the walls. "I don't know. I'm not good with decorating."

"Well. . .you built the house. Surely you must have had some picture in your mind how it would look when completed."

He shrugged. "Actually, I never thought about it that way. I was just focused on finishing it."

Sasha turned back to the wall and held up the wallpaper samples she'd gotten in Tulsa. "All right then, let's go with the floral. It seems more natural than blue for the entry way." She held up the blue again. Maybe she'd use it upstairs in one of the bedrooms.

She peeked at Jim, who stood casually with his hands in his back pockets. "Have you always been a carpenter? You do wonderful work."

His neck and ears took on a reddish tint, and he looked out the tall window next to the front door. "No, actually I've been a farmer most of my life. I learned carpentry on the farm, having to repair and build things, but refined my skills during the Spanish-American War."

Sasha frowned. "How did you learn to be a carpenter during the war?"

Jim's brow dipped, and his lips thinned as he pressed them together. "I was on funeral duty for a while. Built a lot of caskets."

She laid a hand on his arm. "Oh, Jim, I'm so sorry. That must have been difficult."

He nodded and heaved a long sigh. "After that, I didn't want to fight anymore." He glanced at her as if she'd scold him for losing heart.

"I don't blame you. I wouldn't have, either."

"I just kept thinking of the families of those men who were

hoping and praying their fathers, sons, and husbands would come home."

She squeezed his arm. "It must have been horrible for you."

He studied the ground and nodded. "I was threatened with a dishonorable discharge if I didn't fight, but a captain I was friends with stepped in. He got me put on repair detail—fixing wagons, making a structure safe for temporary headquarters. . . stuff like that."

"God was watching over you."

His stunned gaze matched her own surprise at the comment that had spilled from her mouth.

Slowly, his lips turned up in a roguish smile. "I guess He was at that, though I wasn't walking with Him back then. In fact, I was quite a mess for a while after returning home."

"Why didn't you go back to farming after the war?"

He looked out the window again. "I tried, but I was too restless. As much as I wanted to be with my family, it was hard realizing that I'd changed so much while they'd remained the same. I wanted to buy my own land and heard about all the money to be made around here, so I left home and came to Indian Territory."

"Do you plan to buy land around here so you can drill for oil?"

Jim shook his head. "No, I hope to get land closer to my uncle's farm. He lives near Guthrie in the Oklahoma Territory."

Disappointment washed over Sasha. Jim wasn't staying in these parts. When had she started hoping that he might care for her? That they might have a future together?

She licked her lips, knowing she must be a glutton for punishment, but she wanted to prolong her time with him. "So you're not of Indian blood? I thought maybe because of your coloring. . ."

He smiled, lifting her mood. "No, the way I understand it,

we're French and Scottish. I have a grandfather I've never met who owns a big plantation in Georgia."

Sasha fiddled with the samples in her hand. Being French would explain his dark good looks. Still, disappointment raced through her. Jim was the first male friend she'd ever had. Actually, her first true friend. And he didn't seem to mind that she was half Indian, but she couldn't help believing that if he was of native blood, too, he might be more open to a deeper relationship with her. But knowing he was a white man, she doubted he would.

She still felt guilty that he took a beating to help her. His dark bruises had faded to a greenish yellow, and he was getting around well again, but it was her fault he'd been injured.

"You all right?" Jim looked down at her with warm eyes.

She nodded, knowing she had to pull herself out of her mood. Having grown up in a loving family, he wouldn't understand her vital need to hold close those she loved.

Sasha blinked. Did she love Jim?

She gazed up at him. Never having been in love before, how could she know? Turning, she started up the stairs. She needed to get away before he figured out what was wrong. "I'm. . .uh. . .going upstairs to decide what paint and wallpaper I need up there."

"You want help?"

She had to smile at that and looked backed over her shoulder. "I thought you didn't know anything about decorating."

"Aw, you're right. Guess I'll go see what Dewey's up to."

She watched him go out the door and past the window in the entryway. Her heart went with him. How was she supposed to work and eat with him every day without revealing her growing attraction?

twelve

The wagon dipped into a deep rut in the road, knocking Sasha's shoulder against her uncle's. He slapped the reins on the horses' backs, and the animals plodded forward, bringing the wagon back on level ground.

Sasha tightened her grasp on the edge of the seat and thought back to the day she'd been in town, dressed in her costume. If she didn't do something, those men she'd overheard would just keep on swindling the landowners. But who could she trust with the information?

Dewey glanced at her. "Something wrong?"

She nibbled on her lip, wondering how much to tell him. He wouldn't approve of her traipsing around dressed as an old woman and sorting through people's garbage.

"A two-day old stew is mighty good, but stewing over your problems just makes them seem bigger than they are. Why don't you tell me what's bothering you?"

Sasha heaved a sigh and plunged forward. "When I was in town the other day, I overheard some men talking about how Chamber Oil was cheating Indians."

Dewey exhaled a sigh and looked away. After a few moments, he turned back to face her. "I'm aware of their trickery. I know how they dealt with Kizzie. I offered to help her, but the woman had an independent streak as wide as the Arkansas River. She earned a wagonload of money with her oil leases, but it was only a fraction of what she should have made." His eyes darkened with anger. "I have proof she was cheated."

97

"Really? Can't you do anything about it?"

He shook his head. "Not now. Too late."

"It's never too late to right a wrong."

Dewey's kind eyes looked small against his leathery face. "I don't need the money—you know that. I wouldn't mind helping my people to keep them from being cheated though, but I don't know who to trust. The oilmen all seem to be eating from the same bean pot."

"Surely they aren't all bad."

"No, you're right." Dewey shook his head. "But I don't know who I can trust, so I just keep the information to myself. Some landowners have been killed because they refused to sign a lease or wanted more money. I don't need that kind of trouble."

They pulled into Keaton a short while later, and Dewey stopped the wagon under a tree near the train depot. He clambered to the ground, then helped her down.

"I reckon you've got more shopping to do." Dewey smiled. "I know you haven't bought everything we need for that big house yet."

"No, I have a long way to go before I'm done." She studied her uncle for a moment. "Are you sure I'm not spending too much money?"

Smiling, he shook his head. "No, Jim told me how thrifty you're being. I'm proud of you, Sasha. From what he's said, you're buying quality goods but also being frugal."

"Thank you. I'm trying not to spend any more than we need to." Her chest warmed with pride. She'd rarely received such a heartwarming compliment.

"You're doing fine, and I don't want you to worry about it." He patted her shoulder, looking a tad embarrassed. "Now, I need to see if any of that stuff you ordered has arrived." He pulled out his pocket watch and looked at it. "How about if we meet up around half past noon for dinner at the diner?"

"That sounds fine." As they parted, Sasha walked down the boardwalk toward the dressmaker's shop. She hoped the lightweight, front-buttoned dresses she'd ordered were ready. Her New York gowns were too hot and impractical for daily living here.

She rounded the corner and plowed straight into a solid chest. If the man hadn't grabbed her upper arms, she would have plummeted onto her backside. She peeked up to apologize and came face-to-face with—seeing him in person brought the name she hadn't been able to recall a couple of days earlier to mind—Roman Loftus.

"Well, it's a pleasure running into you, Miss Di Carlo." His pearly white smile looked bright against his reddish brown skin. He lifted a derby hat and bowed.

Though embarrassed, she couldn't help smiling at the way he worded his greeting. "Nice running into you, too, although I suppose I should apologize for not paying attention to where I was going."

"No need, I assure you." He waved his hand in the air. "Might I ask where you're headed in such a hurry?"

Sasha's cheeks warmed. "I. . .uh. . .was on my way to do some errands."

"Would you mind if I accompany you? Normally women are perfectly safe in town, but if I were to escort you, then nobody would even consider bothering you."

She preferred being alone, but if his company kept other men away, then maybe she should accept his offer. "Why, yes, Mr. Loftus, I would be happy for you to walk with me."

He offered his arm. "Where to first?"

She slipped her arm through his, giving him a charming smile. "Why the dressmaker's shop, of course."

Mr. Loftus lifted his gaze to the sky and shook his head. "Why doesn't that surprise me?"

"You are free to withdraw your offer."

He patted her arm. "No, no. To the dressmaker's it is."

They strolled along, and she considered how kind he seemed. Could she possibly ask his advice about what she'd overheard? He was an oilman, after all, and might be able to help her. He'd come to Uncle Dewey's aid the other day. But was he trustworthy?

She ducked into the dressmaker's shop, leaving him gladly waiting outside. She paid for the two dresses that were finished and made plans to return the next week for the final garment. As she exited the store, Mr. Loftus tugged at the package in her hand.

"Do allow me to carry this for you." His amiable smile dissolved her objections, and she handed over the parcel.

"Where to now, Miss Di Carlo?"

"Surely you must have some place you need to be."

"No, I have the next few hours free. There's always paperwork to be done, but it can wait for a bit."

They crossed the street, and Sasha pondered whether to confide in him or not. Two women stared at them as they passed in the road. Sasha glanced up at her escort, realizing again how handsome he was. His features, though clearly Indian, were finer than most, giving him a regal air, and he didn't seem the least bit uncomfortable in her company, even though he must be full-blooded Creek.

In the mercantile, she placed an order for some linens from the Montgomery Ward catalog and purchased two sun bonnets like many of the women in town wore. All the while, she wrestled with whether to tell him about the dishonest oilmen or not.

Jim was the one she ought to be confiding in, and she could just imagine his scowl at seeing her on the arm of Roman Loftus. She pushed that thought aside. She needed someone familiar with oil companies and how they worked to help her.

As they exited the store, Mr. Loftus glanced down at her. His dark eyes shimmered with some emotion she couldn't decipher. Could he tell she was a half-breed? Would it matter to him?

"It's well past the noon hour, Miss Di Carlo. Might you consider having lunch with me?"

"Oh my. I'm supposed to meet my uncle at the diner soon. Perhaps you could join us."

He nodded, though she thought he would rather have her to himself. As they approached the diner, she saw Dewey waiting for her near the entrance. He smiled, then studied her escort.

"Afternoon, Mr. Hummingbird." Roman Loftus tipped his hat.

"Mr. Loftus." Dewey pressed his lips together and nodded, then turned to her. "I'm sorry, Sasha, but some of our order just arrived on the noon train. I need to stay at the depot to make sure everything gets unloaded off the train and into our wagon."

She laid her hand on his arm. "It's all right. Mr. Loftus asked me to dine with him. But you won't get to eat."

Dewey waved his hand in the air. "Just have Sue Ann make me a roast beef sandwich and bring it to the depot when you two are done. I should be ready to go by then."

She nodded, and Dewey gave Roman a stern look before leaving. Did her uncle not approve of her escort?

They took their seats, placed an order, and then sat staring at each other. Maybe being with him would help her better understand her feelings for Jim. If she truly cared for Jim, then Mr. Loftus wouldn't hold her interest. But here she was, and as hard as it was to admit, she was curious about the man across from her.

They made small talk for a time. All the while she was getting up her nerve to confide in him. Surely he could help. Soon their food would arrive, and then it would be too late. She leaned forward, and he copied her action.

"Mr. Loftus, I wonder if you might help me with a. . .uh. . . situation."

His dark brows lifted. "Of course, I'd be happy to assist you any way I can."

She looked around to make sure no one was paying them any attention, took a deep breath, and then plunged forward. "I know someone who overheard some men talking about Chamber Oil cheating Indians."

He blinked and looked stunned at her abrupt confession. "This person actually heard this? I mean an actual confession that the oil company is swindling Indians?"

Sasha nodded. "Yes."

"Would this person recognize these men if he saw them again?"

"I don't think so. I don't believe my friend got a good look at them."

He leaned his elbows on the table and steepled his fingers. "Then, unfortunately, there's not much to be done, but I'll ask around and see if I can find out anything. Sadly, many oilmen are unscrupulous, unlike my father and I, who strive to be upright and fair."

"I see." Disappointment flooded Sasha.

"I'm full-blooded Creek and don't like seeing my people getting cheated."

Sasha studied Mr. Loftus as she fiddled with the edge of the tablecloth. There was no doubting his heritage with his straight black hair, dark complexion, and high cheek bones. She no longer remembered why she hadn't wanted to dine with him the other day. Could it be possible that Creeks, beside her uncle, wouldn't be put off by her heritage?

He reached across the table and laid his hand on her forearm.

"Miss Di Carlo, I promise I'll do my best to get to the bottom of this and see that the people involved are punished."

❧

"Move it a little to the right." Sasha watched Jim and a worker push the heavy dresser two inches closer to the bedroom window.

Jim brushed his forehead with his sleeve. "How's that?"

She eyeballed the chest of drawers, deciding it looked perfectly centered between the window and the wall. "That's fine. Thank you."

"All right, we'll bring up the bed frame next." The men trudged into the hall and down the stairs.

Sasha wiped her hand over the walnut highboy dresser, then untied the sash that had held the attached swivel mirror steady during transport. She doubted her uncle had enough clothes to fill it, but at least he wouldn't have to hang things on pegs anymore. The scent of fresh paint still lingered in the room, making her hope her uncle liked the soft blue color. She'd made him stay away until the room was completed, and now excitement and anxiety both swirled in her stomach.

She crossed the room and wiped off the top of the washstand. What she loved most about this small piece of furniture was that the enamel basin could be pulled out for use and pushed in and hidden under the wooden top when not needed. She tugged the basin out and pushed it in.

Jim backed into the room carrying the bed's headboard. "You're not playing with that washstand again, are you?"

Spinning around, she tried to wipe the guilty look off her face. "Just center that along the south wall."

He flashed her a knowing smile, then focused on his job. Her insides tingled at his teasing look.

Several hours later, Sasha's calves ached from climbing the stairs so many times. Her bedroom and her uncle's were complete, and this would be their first night to sleep in the new house.

"I just don't know if I'll be able to sleep in such a big place." Holding an armload of clothes, Dewey looked around his new bedroom. "It's too nice for the likes of me."

Sasha sidled up beside him as Jim came in carrying a wooden chair. "No, it's not. There's nothing fancy in here. Just basic walnut furniture, a quilt, and curtains."

She pointed to the corner where the chair belonged, and Jim set it down. He wiped the back of his hand across his forehead. She could just imagine how tired he must be after lugging furniture upstairs most of the day. Flashing him a smile of gratitude, she turned back to her uncle.

Dewey shook his head. "Looks mighty fancy to me. But you did a fine job, and I'm proud of you."

She was having the time of her life supplying the house and making it livable, and Dewey's comment gave her a sense of satisfaction that she'd rarely felt before. Deep in her heart, she hoped she never had to return to New York.

❧

A warm sense of admiration surged through Jim as he watched Sasha light up at Dewey's comment. Her uncle was right— she had done a wonderful job so far of outfitting the house. Dewey's bedroom was simple but nice. Sasha's room was a bit more elegant, but still usable and practical. The rose carpeting matched the design on her bedding and the sheer curtains that covered the window.

He loved seeing Sasha's eyes light up. They reminded him of coffee with just a drip of cream. Wisps of rebellious hairs had pulled free from her long braid and danced about her face whenever the wind whipped in the open window.

Blowing out a sigh, he knew he needed to walk down the hill and head to bed, but he was so tired from hauling furniture upstairs all day, he didn't want to move.

"Well, Jimmy, I reckon you can sleep in the cabin tonight."

Jim's heart skipped a beat. "Are you sure? You haven't gotten all your belongings out yet." He wouldn't admit that sleeping on the cabin's bed sounded much more inviting than spending the night on the stiff cot in his tent.

Dewey nodded. "Yep, I'm sure. It's time we called it a night. We're all tuckered out from working so hard, though I don't know how I'll sleep in this fancy bed."

Sasha gave Dewey a kiss on the cheek, waved good night to Jim, then walked down the hall to her room. Jim longed for her to kiss him, too, but he bid them good night and shuffled down the stairs, wishing for once that the cabin wasn't so far away. Parts of his body were still tender from the beating he'd taken, and after today's workout, he longed for a soak in a hot tub. The creek would have to do though.

As he stepped out into the warm evening, he couldn't get Sasha's lovely face out of his mind. She was beautiful inside and out. She already loved Dewey, and Jim felt sure that she cared for him, too. He longed to get to know her better and deepen their friendship.

But could there be any future for him and a woman of Indian heritage? It wouldn't be the first time for an Indian and white man to court and maybe marry. In fact, there were many such marriages in the Twin Territories, but what would his family say to such a union?

What would Sasha say?

thirteen

Sasha wiped down the buffet cabinet with beeswax. As she moved her flannel rag back and forth, her gaze darted over to where Jim was attaching the legs to the oak dining table that he had just brought inside. With the sleeves of his chambray shirt rolled up, she could see the muscles in his forearm contract as he attached the leg to the table. Sighing, she refocused on her job.

She loved to watch Jim work. He was so meticulous in all that he did. She was sure he'd never done a job halfway in all his life. He was nice-looking, honest, and had a faith in God she admired.

She peeked at him again, and his eyes locked onto hers. A warm blush heated her cheeks at being caught staring. Jim's eyes sparkled. He smiled, then winked at her.

Stifling a gasp at his forwardness, she concentrated again on her polishing. Butterflies danced in her stomach, and she marveled that she'd never met a man who stirred her like he did. She sighed again, wishing, hoping there could be a future for them. But Jim said he planned to move back to the Oklahoma Territory, and now that she had a home and an uncle who loved her, she wasn't about to leave—even if Jim was willing to marry an Indian. She loved her uncle—even though he wasn't refined and sophisticated like her mother's friends—and they were family.

Jim chuckled, making her turn around again. "You're doing some mighty heavy sighing over there. Must be thinking awful hard."

She opened her mouth to correct him but knew he spoke the truth.

"I'm always willing to listen if you need someone to talk to."

Wasn't that just like him? Considerate to the core. But there was no way she could tell Jim that she'd been thinking about him.

"That's done." He stood and stretched, nearly popping the buttons off his shirt.

Her mouth went dry. She longed to lean against his solid chest and have his arms wrap around her.

She shook her head. What was wrong with her? She was acting like an enamored school girl. Everett, Jim's helper, walked in carrying two of the chairs that matched the table. Sasha was grateful for the distraction. "Just put those along the wall for now."

He did as she asked, then helped Jim turn the table onto its legs.

Jim looked at her. "Where do you want it?"

She waved her hand in the air. "Put it in front of the double windows, but leave about three feet so we can put the chairs in. We'll enjoy a nice view of the field when we eat in here."

The men did as told, and she marveled at how lovely the room looked with the furniture in it. The floral wallpaper that Jim and Everett had put up several days ago brightened the room and added a rainbow of color. She picked up a chair and slid it under the table, wondering if life could get any better.

"I'll get the other chairs." Everett disappeared into the hallway.

Sasha glanced at Jim as he retrieved the matching chair. She imagined him sitting at the head of the table with her beside him, eating together every day. Yes, it was possible that life could get better. If only. . .

A knock sounded on the front door, pulling Sasha from her work. She hurried to the front of the house, eager to see who their first official visitor was. She pushed open the screen door and saw Roman Loftus dressed in a dark brown, three-piece suit standing off to the side, staring down at the pond. His horse grazed nearby. Mr. Loftus turned and smiled.

"Good day, Miss Di Carlo." He tipped his hat and looked past her. "Mighty fine place your uncle has here."

Sasha smiled, delighted to have someone to show the house to. "Would you like to see the inside?"

"Yes, I would. Thank you."

She stepped back, and he entered, closing the screen without letting it bang. That small feat impressed her, because Jim had been going in and out for days, banging the door each time. She relieved him of his hat and laid it on the entryway table. When she looked back, she noticed him admiring the curved staircase.

"Very nice indeed."

"Yes, Jim Conners and his workers have done a beautiful job."

Mr. Loftus's brows dipped down for a moment. "Ah, so that's what he does around here. I'd wondered."

Sasha ignored his comment about Jim and held out her hand, indicating for him to enter the parlor. "The furniture for this room hasn't arrived yet, so I can't offer you a place to sit—unless you'd care to move to the dining room."

"No, thank you. I actually came out to talk to you about something."

Her heart skittered as she placed her hand against her chest. "Did you find out who those men were?"

He pressed his lips into a straight line. "No, sorry. I haven't had any luck on that account."

Disappointment sagged her shoulders. "Oh, I'd hoped you had. It's a very serious thing."

"I haven't given up, I assure you." He studied her face, and his countenance seemed to brighten. "I was wondering. . . . Natalie Carmichael is coming to Tulsa next weekend. Have you heard of her?"

"Oh, yes. She has a reputation as a wonderful opera singer, though I've never heard her perform."

Mr. Loftus looped his thumbs in his lapels and hung on. "Then you must accompany me to hear her."

Sasha blinked, stunned that he'd asked her to go with him to Tulsa. Her thoughts flew to Jim, and she found herself wishing he was the one asking her out. But he wasn't, and probably never would. She needed Mr. Loftus's help in tracking down the dishonest oilmen, and it would be wise to stay in his good graces.

"Miss Carmichael is doing a two o'clock matinee, so we could have dinner, attend the program, and still get back home before dark—thanks to the train."

As she wrestled with what to do, Jim walked in, carrying an armload of window blinds that he had picked up at the Keaton depot. The screen door banged shut, making Sasha wince. Jim stopped quickly and scowled when Roman Loftus stepped out of the parlor. The two men stared each other down like a couple of rams about to butt heads.

Finally, Jim nodded. "Afternoon. If you're looking for Mr. Hummingbird, he's down at the cabin getting some of his belongings."

Mr. Loftus smiled like he was the only rooster in the hen-house. "I found who I was looking for."

Jim's dark brows dipped as he looked from Sasha to Mr. Loftus and back. "I reckon I'll get back to work if you don't need me."

His comment was directed at Sasha, and she shook her head, giving him a gentle smile. She could read his curiosity but knew his good manners would keep him from lingering. He nodded and started up the stairs, looking back over his shoulder.

"So, what do you think? Would you have dinner and go to the show with me?"

Sasha heard Jim stumble at the top of the stairs. Her heart jumped to her throat, and she looked up to be sure he was all right. He stood on the landing, glaring down. He looked fine, but not too happy.

Maybe he was jealous of Mr. Loftus's attention. She turned back to face her visitor, certain that he'd just wiped a smirk off his face. If she didn't need his help, she never would have considered his offer. But she did.

"Yes, I do believe I'd like that, Mr. Loftus."

His brilliant smile could have lit up the whole room. "Wonderful. But since we'll be seeing more of each other, you must call me Roman."

"We'll see," she said, smiling wryly. She wasn't sure that she wanted to take that step so soon.

"I'll pick you up at ten o'clock on Saturday. That should give us plenty of time to get to Tulsa and have dinner before the show." He headed for the front door, picked up his hat, and then cast a victorious glance upstairs.

She escorted him outside and waved as he rode off. Was she doing the right thing? If she'd said no to his offer, would he still have been willing to help her?

Well. . .she'd never know the answer to that question now. As she went back inside, she looked upstairs, but Jim wasn't in sight. Somehow she felt sure he'd be displeased with her.

And she didn't like that feeling one bit.

❧

Jim wanted to slam the blinds onto the floor, but he resisted. It made his heart ache to know that Sasha was going out on the town with Roman Loftus. The thought of her alone with the slimy oilman made his stomach churn.

Couldn't she tell that he had feelings for her? But then he hadn't exactly made his intentions known—partly because he wasn't sure what they were. All he knew was that Sasha was special, and when he was near her, his whole being felt as if he'd grabbed onto an electric light fixture the wrong way.

Jim picked up a blind and unwrapped the paper covering it. He was certain that Roman was just another oilman looking for a way to make more money. It didn't matter that he was Creek; he was still an oilman watching out for his own interests first.

He crossed the room, checked his measurements and the number on the blind to make sure he had the correct one, and then unwound the string that was wrapped around it. He clenched his jaw, concerned about Sasha's safety.

Seeing movement outside, he felt his ire rise as he watched Roman Loftus ride off. The man had put down a silent challenge with the looks he'd cast Jim when Sasha wasn't watching. He had a sneaky suspicion the man was using Sasha to get to Dewey.

Jim leaned the shade against the wall and paced the guest bedroom. He had to face the truth that he cared for Sasha— maybe even loved her—but he had nothing to offer besides a little money in the bank.

He sighed and rubbed the back of his neck. He could never compete with the lifestyle Sasha had lived her whole life. If they ever married, how could he ask her to leave her uncle when she'd just gotten to know and love him? And what about this house that she'd put so much time and effort into? Would she leave all this to live in a soddy with him?

Frustrated, he stomped down the stairs and out the front door, relishing the loud slam the screen made. With Sasha being Dewey's only living relative other than her mother, whenever he died, she would most likely inherit his wealth.

He'd gotten his hopes up about a relationship with her, and now he was paying the price.

There was no way to bridge the differences in their lives.

He didn't even have a home or land of his own, and here Sasha was living in a brand-new house—a fancy one, at that.

The painful truth drove him, and he had to get away. He jogged down the hill to his horse, tossed on the saddle, and rode off at top speed. The wind whipped his face, along with an occasional insect. His horse's hooves pounded out a rhythm he couldn't get out of his head.

You can't have her. You can't have her.

fourteen

On Saturday afternoon, Jim reined his horse to a stop. Three hours of riding fence lines, checking for breaks, hadn't erased the picture of Sasha leaving in the wagon with Roman Loftus. The man had resembled a gloating rooster who'd swallowed the biggest insect in the pen as he escorted Sasha to his buggy. And Sasha—she looked like a princess all dressed up in her shimmering blue gown. All satin and lace.

Jim's jaw ached from being clenched so much the past few hours. He was angry at Loftus for asking Sasha to Tulsa. Angry at her for accepting. And angry for not being honest with Sasha and himself.

Swatting at a mosquito, he considered why he'd been hesitant to approach her about his feelings. Besides their differences, there was her Indian blood.

He smacked his leg, angry at himself that he had been prejudiced—even a little bit. Why did it matter? He was of mixed blood himself—part French, part Scot, and who knows what else.

He was a Christian, and bloodlines shouldn't matter. People were created in God's image—equal and valuable—and should be judged on their character and what they did with their lives, not on who their ancestors were.

Of all people, he shouldn't care about bloodlines. Dewey Hummingbird was one of the finest men he'd known. He'd helped Jim become a stronger Christian and helped him overcome his anger and frustrations from fighting in the war.

Maybe what really bothered him was that he had so little to offer Sasha—and he'd used her heritage as a crutch to keep him from facing that fact.

He came to a creek and checked the water for oil seepage before letting his horse drink. Many cattle in the area had died from drinking water that oil had seeped into, but Dewey had been blessed not to lose any of his.

He spent the next hour praying and seeking God as he headed back to the cabin. Finally, his heart found peace. He would confess his feelings to Sasha and let the Lord work things out. A smile tugged at his cheeks for the first time since he'd learned about Sasha's dinner outing with Loftus.

As he rode over the hill, past the new house, his heart stopped. A cloud of black smoke boiled into the sky near where the cabin was.

Fire!

He dug his heels into his mount and galloped down the hill. His heart melted as he saw the cabin in flames, and ten feet away, Dewey lay on the ground, badly beaten. Both eyes were swollen shut, his lip was split, and his arm looked busted.

Jim leaped off his horse while it was still moving and skidded to a stop beside Dewey. Kneeling, his gaze roamed over his friend's battered body. Anger battled pain. Who would do such a thing to a kind, old man?

He carefully lifted Dewey by the shoulders and dragged him away from the fire, wincing when his mentor moaned.

"Jim. . ." Dewey lifted a bloody hand. "Oilmen. . .attacked me. . . . I wouldn't sign their lease."

"Shhh. . .rest now. We'll talk later." Jim patted Dewey's shoulder, hoping there'd be a later.

Dewey clutched Jim's sleeve. "Have evidence. . .Chamber Oil cheating Creeks. . .in box in cabin."

Jim glanced at the blazing cabin. It shuddered, and the

roof collapsed with a loud roar, sending fiery debris and ash sprinkling down around them. Whatever evidence had been inside no longer existed, but he couldn't tell Dewey that.

Tears—probably from the smoke and ash—stung his eyes. He brushed the back of his hand across them.

"Jim, I love you. . .like a son. Take care of Sasha." Life seeped out of Dewey, and he went limp.

Jim heaved a sob and brushed his hand over his friend's dark hair. He loved this old man and would dearly miss him. Tears streamed down his cheeks as he gently lifted Dewey, carried him into the barn, and laid him in the wagon bed.

How would he ever break the news to Sasha that her beloved uncle was dead?

მ

"So, did you have an enjoyable time?" Roman put his arm along the back of the train seat and turned sideways to face her.

She looked up at him and smiled. "I had a delightful time. Thank you for asking me. The singer was wonderful, as well as the meal." Even though she had been nervous, she'd had a magnificent time. Perhaps there were some things she missed about New York.

"Good, I'm glad. Maybe we can do it again sometime."

"Perhaps." Sasha gave him a shy smile. Roman had been polite and charming all day.

"I have to admit, I still don't understand why your uncle doesn't want to lease his land. People would kill for such an opportunity."

A shudder charged through her at his sudden change in conversation. Sasha stared out the window at the landscape whizzing by. "My uncle has enough money to satisfy him and wants to preserve his land."

Roman chuckled and shook his head. "How can anyone ever have enough money?"

"It's more than the money—his land is his home, and he doesn't want it defiled."

"Land is land. He could lease his and buy a huge ranch somewhere else with all the money he'd make. He could have the best of both worlds and be unbelievably rich, too."

Sasha sighed, truly uncomfortable for the first time all day. In spite of being full-blooded Creek, Roman couldn't understand that sometimes owning land that family has lived on for years was more important than becoming wealthy.

He waved his hand in the air. "Never mind. I'm sorry for throwing a wet blanket on our lovely day. Let's not talk any more business."

She leaned back in her seat, relieved. Still, she couldn't help being disappointed with his attitude. But he was an oilman— so what else should she expect but that he'd talk oil?

In the back of her mind, she couldn't help wondering if he'd asked her to dinner just to try to persuade her to his way of thinking.

Well, it wouldn't work, if that was his plan.

Her thoughts drifted to Jim. What was he doing right now? He'd looked both hurt and angry when she left with Roman. She dipped her brow. Well, so what. He didn't return her affections, so he had no say in what she did. His opinion didn't matter one whit.

As much as she wanted to believe that, her heart told her it wasn't true.

※

Sasha paced the depot, her footsteps echoing on the wooden planks of the floor. Roman had gone to retrieve the buggy from the livery and would be returning any minute. He'd asked her to dinner next Saturday, and she needed to give him an answer. Part of her wanted to say yes, but another part didn't.

"Sasha."

She whirled around, surprised to hear Jim's voice. His filthy face looked as if it were covered in coal dust, and he reeked of smoke. He stood there with his hat in his hand, gazing on her with a miserable expression on his face.

"What are you doing here?" She couldn't help wondering if he was spying on her and Roman.

Before he could answer, Roman approached, his brows tucked down. "You couldn't wait until I got her home to talk to her?" His haughty gaze took in Jim's disheveled appearance, and he smirked.

Jim pinned Roman with a pointed glare, then his gaze softened to apologetic as he looked at her. "Sasha. . ." He glanced away, but when he turned back, his eyes glimmered with unshed tears, sending a shaft of fear straight to her heart. "There's been an accident. Dewey. . .is dead."

Sasha gasped as a pang of grief threatened to knock her off her feet. "No, it can't be. What happened?"

Her knees turned to butter, and her head buzzed. She reached out and grabbed hold of Jim's forearm. He looked as if he wanted to hold her, but then he glanced at her clothes and then his.

"The cabin was set on fire, and somebody beat up your uncle."

She sagged, and both men reached for her, but Jim grabbed her first.

"C'mon over here and sit down. Loftus, get her some water."

Roman scowled, obviously not used to being bossed around, but left anyway.

"Dewey told me it was oilmen, trying to force him into signing."

Tears coursed down Sasha's face as she thought of her dear uncle hurting and now dead while she was off having a good time.

Jim handed her a dingy handkerchief. "Sorry, it's clean but smells like smoke."

She shrugged but accepted it and wiped her face and nose. "I can't believe it came to this."

"Me, neither. I talked with the sheriff, but since there were no witnesses except Dewey, there's not much he can do. I told him about the three men who'd been pressuring Dewey, and he said he'd check them out."

Sasha jumped up, her dress swishing. "There has to be something he can do. People can't commit murder and get away with it."

Roman returned with her water, and she downed the whole cupful.

"Let me take you home," Roman said. "You've had quite a shock."

Jim shook his head. "I'll take her."

Roman looked ready for a battle, but Sasha laid her hand on his arm. "There's no sense in you driving clear to the ranch when Jim's already here. I had a wonderful time and thank you for it." She pinned on a no-argument stare.

"But—" Roman opened his mouth to protest, then slammed it shut. He glared at Jim, then bowed to her. "Thank you for accompanying me today. It would be my pleasure to escort you again once you're feeling better." Spinning around, he stalked toward the buggy.

Sasha hated refusing him after he'd been so nice all day and had spent so much money on her, but at the moment, the only person she wanted to be with was Jim. He loved her uncle as much or even more than she, and he understood her agony and grief in a way Roman never could.

fifteen

On the way home, Jim pulled the wagon to a stop where the road diverged, one way leading to the new house and the other to the cabin.

"Are you sure about this?"

Sasha nodded, then dabbed her nose again with Jim's handkerchief. "I need to see it."

"It's just a burned down cabin."

She waved her hand to the left. "Just go. Please."

The overwhelming since of loss she felt as the cabin came into view a few minutes later threatened to knock her off the buggy seat.

Her uncle was gone.

And now she was alone. Again.

Smoke still drifted up, and embers glowed in the debris that once was her uncle's cabin. Ashes drifted like black snow on the light afternoon breeze. Her hopes and dreams floated away with them.

"Seen enough?" Jim asked, his voice laced with compassion.

She nodded, and he clucked to the horses, which moved away at a quick pace, obviously happy to be away from the heat of the debris.

Numb, she watched a waddling mother duck lead her ducklings into the pond as they passed. As they rode up the hill, the house came into view. She sniffed and held back a sob. Such a big, beautiful house, and she alone would live there now.

She looked down at her ruined dress. Soot from Jim's clothing had turned the pale blue gown gray. It was just as well, because she knew she would never wear it again. She'd been off having a gay time while her uncle had suffered and died. The dress would only remind her that she should have been here. Maybe she could have made a difference.

Jim pulled the wagon to a stop in front of the house and came around to help her down. As he set her on the ground, all her pain and fears came gushing out, and she burst into tears. "What will I do without him?"

⁂

Sharing Sasha's blinding pain, Jim pulled her into his arms. Her dress was already ruined, so he no longer worried about that. He ran his hand over her soft hair and held her head against his chest. She sobbed and moaned with grief, her tears bleeding through his shirt.

Against his will, Jim's own tears streamed forth. He'd miss his old friend more than anyone he'd ever lost.

Finally, Sasha stepped back a half step, but Jim kept her in the circle of his arms. He loved this woman and wanted to protect her. She glanced up, looking so pitiful with her red, splotchy face and moist eyelashes. "What am I going to do?"

He wiped away her tears with his thumbs and tried to smile. "You'll go on living—here in Dewey's house. He built it for you, you know."

Sasha blinked, looking confused.

"He told me just last week that he'd promised his sister to build a fine house so that when you and your mother came to visit, y'all would have a nice place to stay. He said he'd never given up hope and knew you'd come one day."

Sasha's chin and lower lip quivered. A fresh set of tears escaped.

Jim knew he shouldn't take advantage of her grief, but he couldn't have stopped if a hundred horses held him back. He lowered his face and kissed her, hoping to comfort her. Needing her comfort.

For a brief moment, she just stood there, then she wrapped her arms around his neck and returned his kiss.

Oh, how he loved this woman and wanted to protect her and see her happy. Finally, needing air, he pulled away. A smile tugged at his lips. "I'm afraid I got your face dirty."

A fiery rose blush glowed through the soot and tears. "It's all right. I'm a mess anyway."

He tugged at her hands. "C'mon. Let's get you inside." He escorted her upstairs and stopped in the hall outside her room. "Will you be all right while I get some fresh water so you can clean up?"

She nodded, but the look she gave him was like a puppy that had lost its master. He took her face in his hands and stared deeply in her eyes. "We'll get through this—together."

*

The next morning, Jim paced the entryway to the back of the house, willing Sasha to come down. He hadn't wanted to leave her alone but knew he couldn't sleep under the same roof, so he'd pitched his tent in the backyard. But sleep had eluded him. He couldn't get Dewey's battered body or Sasha's distraught expression out of his mind.

A creak on the stairs alerted him to Sasha's presence. She glided down, dressed in a gray cotton work dress. She flashed him an embarrassed smile and looked at her skirt. "I don't have anything black to wear."

Jim's heart ached for her. "Dewey wouldn't want you to wear mourning clothes."

She shrugged and walked past him into the kitchen. "Thanks

for making coffee. I sure need it today."

She poured a cup and sat at the kitchen table. Jim pulled a plate of scrambled eggs and bacon off the back burner and set it on the table in front of her.

"I don't think I can eat a thing."

The chair squeaked as Jim pulled it away from the table and sat. "You need to keep up your strength. We. . .uh. . .have to go to town and take care of the funeral arrangements."

Sasha's lower lip quivered.

"I can do it alone if you don't want to."

Her gaze darted up. "No, I need to have a part. It's the least I can do for Uncle Dewey."

Jim picked up the fork and stabbed a piece of egg. "Here, eat this."

She looked at it and shook her head. Jim ignored her resistance and held the bite against her mouth. She peeked up at him, a red blush staining her cheeks, and then she opened her mouth and took the bite.

"I've been thinking. You shouldn't stay here alone." Jim tapped the table while she ate. "I moved my tent to the backyard in case you need me, but you really should have a woman here with you."

Sasha shook her head. "I'll be fine by myself."

"I know it's none of my business, but I was thinking maybe you could help out an oil widow or two and yourself at the same time."

Her eyes sparkled at his comment. "You know, that might not be a bad idea."

≈

Sasha stood in front of Mary McMurphey, trying hard not to wring her hands. The widow had seemed defensive when Sasha asked her if she'd like to come work for her.

"I don't know, ma'am. It's a far piece to travel, and I'd hate to leave my children all day."

"My foreman, Jim Conners"—Sasha waved a hand toward the buggy—"can build a room on the back of the house where you can live with your children."

Something flickered in Mary's eyes. Hope maybe? Then they dulled. "But I would still have to leave them alone all day, ma'am. Here, everyone watches out for the children."

Sasha felt herself losing ground. "Well, the fact is, I could use two people. Someone to tend the house and another person to cook. Would you happen to know someone who is a good cook who might have an older child that could keep the children during the day? I wouldn't mind paying her a little something for the chore."

Sasha could tell the wheels in Mary's mind were churning. She was certain she'd made headway.

Mary looked across the ragged tent city, and Sasha followed her gaze. A thin woman stood holding a toddler while a teenage girl brushed her hair.

"Rita is a mighty fine cook, and she lost her husband a few months back."

"Do you think she'd be interested in employment?"

Mary nodded. "I reckon she would. She's got three young'uns to feed."

The blond urchin Sasha remembered from the festival skipped over and wrapped her arms around Mary's skirt. "Who's she, Mama? Her dress is purdy."

"Miss Di Carlo, ma'am, this here's my daughter, Leah. She's my oldest. My son, Philip, is around somewhere."

Sasha stooped down and held out her hand to the little girl. "A pleasure to meet you, Leah."

The child giggled, then glanced at her mother. When Mary

nodded, Leah shook Sasha's hand. Straightening, Sasha looked at Mary again. "So do we have a deal? I can pay you ten dollars a week and provide you with a room of your own and all the food your family can eat."

Mary's eyes widened. "It's far too much, ma'am."

"I disagree. I desperately need the help and wouldn't mind the companionship. My offer is the same for Rita. You'll talk to her?"

Mary finally smiled. "Yes, ma'am, I surely will. And I'd be honored to accept the position. When should I start?"

Sasha figured it would take Jim several weeks to finish the room but hated to think of Mary and her children living in such squalor till then. "What if you pack up your things, and I'll send Jim to fetch you in two days. You can set up your tent in my backyard and live there until he finishes your room."

"That sounds just fine and dandy, ma'am. I'll work hard. You won't be sorry for giving me this chance."

"I have no doubts that you will, and I look forward to getting to know you and your family better."

Jim hopped off the wagon as Sasha approached. Her heart lurched at the smile on his face.

"Was she interested?"

"Yes, after I convinced her how much I needed her assistance. And she's going to ask her friend if she'd like to be the cook."

"You did a good thing today, Sasha. I'm proud of you."

She beamed at him as she thought of the two rooms he would have to build, which meant he'd have to stay a while longer. "Yes, I think I did. Thank you for suggesting it."

He helped her up, then took his seat again. He slapped the reins on the mare's back, and the buggy lurched forward. "You might need to buy another buggy and a horse so the women can get to work. It would be too far to walk twice a day, and I won't have time to pick them up and bring them back everyday."

"I...uh...told Mary that you'd build her and the cook rooms of their own behind the house."

Jim glanced at her, looking serious. "Did you, now?"

Sasha nodded, hoping he wouldn't mind. "I didn't think they'd feel comfortable living upstairs with me."

"Guess I'll just have to hang around for a while then." The smile he gave her set her heart stampeding.

"I guess you will."

As they drove home, Sasha savored her success. She'd have help with the house and would be assisting two of the oil widows and their children. Not to mention Jim would have to stay longer since he now had two more bedrooms to build.

Jim had been there for her since Dewey's death and seemed comfortable around her—at least until he'd kissed her. Now he seemed to avoid her unless she needed him for something. Was it because he never could think of her as more than a friend? Did he regret kissing her?

She had compared Roman and Jim again and again, and every time, Jim won hands down. But did it really matter? She might have to return to New York soon. Uncle Dewey had said his property would be hers when he was gone, but no one expected him to be gone this quickly. Maybe she should reconsider building those extra rooms.

Jim guided the buggy down the road toward home, but at the fork, he turned the horse toward town. Sasha peeked sideways at him.

"We have to go in to Keaton and make funeral arrangements." He pressed his lips together in a sympathetic smile.

The joys of the day leaked away like milk in a cracked jar.

sixteen

The day after her visit to Rag Town, Sasha allowed Jim to escort her away from the small church. It had touched her heart that so many people had turned out for her uncle's funeral. Mary and Rita, along with several other oil widows, offered their condolences, and Mary had handed her a fresh-baked loaf of pan bread.

She clung to Jim's arm as they walked down the hill. Sweat trickled down her back from the warm sun. Sparrows chirped and flittered happily in the nearby trees, oblivious to her pain.

She'd only known her uncle a short time but had loved him dearly. Her heart ached to think she'd never see his twinkling eyes or receive another hug from him again. Using her lace handkerchief, she dabbed at her eyes, knowing they must be red and puffy. Jim patted her arm and gave her a reassuring smile.

A shadow darkened their path. Sasha tore her gaze away from Jim and saw Roman standing in their way, his hat in his hands.

"I'm terribly sorry about your uncle. I've talked with the sheriff, and he's using all his resources to find out who attacked him."

Jim tucked her a bit closer to him. She didn't fuss about his protectiveness but rather appreciated it.

Roman's dark brows dipped. "If there's anything I can do to help you, please don't hesitate to call on me."

"Thank you. That's kind of you." She smiled and stepped

around Roman, only wanting to return to the quiet of Dewey's house. But they still had to take her uncle's body back to the ranch and bury him in the family plot. She didn't have the strength within her today to deal with Jim and Roman fussing like two dogs over one bone.

She spotted the wagon parked in the shade of an elm tree and made a beeline for it. Soon they'd be back home, and she needed to decide what to do. Here she'd gone and gotten up Mary and Rita's hopes for a better life and asked Jim to stay and build their rooms, yet she had no idea if she even had a right to stay and live on Dewey's property. Jim had suggested looking for a will before, but she'd been too disheartened to consider it.

Almost to the wagon, Jim stopped suddenly, pulling on her arm. She looked up to see the three men who'd accosted her uncle on several occasions standing near the buggy. She shook her head and heaved a sigh. They were the last people she wanted to see today. In fact, she believed in her heart that these men were responsible for her uncle's death.

The trio lined up, blocking the path to their buggy. The short, heavy-set man tipped his hat to her, looking like a fat cat who'd captured a mouse. "We were right sorry to hear about your uncle, ma'am." The sickeningly sweet smile he flashed made Sasha's stomach churn.

Tall Man stepped forward, looking pleased with himself. A wary premonition charged down her spine, raising tiny bumps on her arms. "I'm sorry to be the one to inform you of this on the day of your uncle's funeral, but Dewey Hummingbird willed all his property to the town of Keaton in the event of his death."

Numb with shock, she clutched Jim's arm like a lifeline. She peeked up and saw the same astonishment on his face that she felt.

Jim stepped forward, setting her behind him. "I don't believe that for one second."

Tall Man opened his hands and held them out, palms up. "I'm afraid it's the truth. Dewey had no relatives except you and your mother, and since he hadn't heard from you in years, he decided to leave his property to the town."

Jim's hands rested on his hips, his back rigid. "I still don't believe that. What proof do you have?"

"It's common knowledge. There was big talk all over Keaton after he'd filed his will with the town attorney." Tall Man hiked his chin, rocked back on his heels, and gloated.

"We'll just see about that." Jim's fist clenched, and then he swiveled toward her, taking her hand and pulling her with him. "Let's go talk with the attorney."

"You have two weeks to pack up and clear out." Tall Man's victorious shout made Sasha shudder. How could this be happening?

She took two steps to each of Jim's, trying to keep up. "Do you think that's true? That Uncle Dewey left his land to the town?"

Jim glanced at her. "No, I don't, but without his will, we can't prove it. I can't see the town knowing Dewey's business anyway. He wouldn't have mentioned what was in his will, nor would the attorney."

"Do you have any idea where he might have put it?"

"I don't know. Maybe his new room?" Jim rubbed his hand along his nape and peered at her. "I just hope it wasn't in the cabin."

Two weeks to clear out. What would she do? Since her uncle had put her name on the bank account, she had plenty of money, but she didn't particularly want to return to New York. She wasn't even sure if she'd still have a job with the theater troupe. Geoffrey hadn't been happy when she'd left, right on her mother's tail. He'd wanted her to take Cybil's place.

She probably wouldn't have to work, at least not for a long while, but she needed something to occupy her time. Maybe she could start over somewhere else.

But where?

She dreaded the thought of leaving her new home. She'd finally found a place to put down roots, but it was being stolen away from her.

Jim's steps slowed in front of the attorney's office, and he reached for the door knob. When he lowered his hand, Sasha noticed the cardboard sign affixed to the window. Gone on holiday. Will return on July 16.

She glanced at Jim. "But that's three weeks from now! What are we going to do?"

A muscle in his jaw ticked. "We go home and find that will."

❧

"It's not here." Sasha flopped onto her uncle's bed, looking dejected. "Where could Uncle Dewey have hidden his will?"

Jim wanted to wrap his arms around her and comfort her, but he kept his distance. They had too many other things to worry about right now and didn't need to complicate the situation with romance. He pulled out the lone chair in Dewey's new bedroom, spun it around, and sat on it backwards. Leaning his arms on the top, he surveyed the messy room. Drawers hung open where they'd searched through Dewey's meager supply of clothing. Even the bedding was askew from their quest.

"I don't know where else to look." Sasha stopped crushing the bedcovers in her fist and looked at him. "Do you know of any secret hiding places he had?"

Jim shook his head, wishing he did. "No. If he had such a place, it was most likely in the cabin."

"Maybe we should search through the ashes. Something might have survived."

"Good idea." He offered her a weak smile. He didn't want to get her hopes up, but at the same time, he didn't want to discourage her. She'd already lost her uncle, and now she could well lose the home she'd put so much effort into.

Sasha slid to her feet and walked toward the door. "I'll go make us some dinner, and then we can go check the cabin—and maybe the barn, too."

Jim sighed as she exited the room, wishing he could help her more. What would happen to her if they couldn't find the will? Would Sasha return to New York?

He stood and swung the chair back into the corner, knowing his heart would break if that happened. He shoved his hands into his back pockets, and his fingers rattled some paper.

The letter.

In all the commotion of the funeral, the confrontation with the three men, and burying Dewey, he'd forgotten about the letter from his uncle that he'd picked up at the post office earlier. Jim pulled the envelope from his pocket and tore it open with his finger.

Dear Jimmy,

I can't tell you how happy it made me to hear that you are satisfied with your job. Dewey Hummingbird sounds like a fine man, and I'm glad that he's been an encouragement in your walk with the Lord. I had my doubts when you left the farm last, but God was directing you to where you needed to be.

I have some news. My father died. He left me his plantation in Georgia, but I don't yet know what I'll do with it. I have no desire to ever live there again. Only bad memories surface when I think of that place.

I know I should grieve over my father's death, but the truth is, he was a cruel man, and my only grief comes from knowing he didn't walk with God.

Father sent me a letter last year when he learned he was dying. I've wrestled with whether to share his deathbed confession with you or not. But given your circumstances and surroundings, I thought you'd want to know.

All my life, I was told that my grandmother, my father's mother, had come from France. She had fine, dark features and looked like a porcelain doll. I never questioned that, but it seems our family sheltered a secret—grandmother was in truth a full-blooded Creek Indian. Back in those days you were a pariah if you married an Indian. It's amazing the secret was kept for so long.

I hope this information doesn't dishearten you. I admit it was a shock at first, but there are many fine people who are of mixed blood. And to God, we are all the same anyhow.

Come back home when you can. We all miss you. Dusty and Katie are doing fine, and Joey is getting big. Bet you miss playing with him. Being an uncle is a fun job, isn't it?

Yours always,
Uncle Mason

Jim's arms fell to his lap as if they bore lead weights. He blinked as he tried to absorb his uncle's letter. Here he'd wrestled with being attracted to a half-breed woman, and he was himself at least one-eighth Creek Indian.

He let out a laugh at the irony of it all.

ॐ

Sasha watched Jim pace off the outline of the rooms he was going to build for Mary and Rita. Long, lean legs ate up the distance in short measure. Jim glanced her way. She'd struggled with what to do, but Jim had encouraged her to move ahead and not let their problems change things. He believed with all his heart they'd find the will and that God would work everything out. And she wanted to believe that, too.

"Are you sure you want two rooms for each worker?"

She nodded. "Originally, I just thought to build one room, but both women have children. They need a place to call home, and one room just isn't enough."

He pushed his hat off his forehead. "Honestly, I think it might work better if we build some cabins out in those trees, rather than adding on to the house." He pointed to a cluster of pine trees.

Sasha pushed away from the house and followed him. "That's not a bad idea. It would give them some privacy. Although, in bad weather, they'd have to brave the elements to get to the big house."

"True." He walked around, studying the area. "Well, what if we put them here?" He stood in a spot halfway between the pine trees and the house.

Sasha considered it, glancing at the house and then the trees. "No, I think it would work better if you build the cabins near the pines. It's really not all that far—"

She spun around at the sound of hoofbeats. Roman rode along the east side of the house on a pretty roan. Sasha wasn't sure if she was happy to see him or not. The time alone with Jim was special, and Roman seemed like an intruder. As long as she and Jim stayed busy, she didn't grieve as deeply as when she just sat around thinking.

Roman scowled when he saw Jim but reined his horse to a stop and vaulted off. When his gaze landed on her, his smile turned charming. He approached her with bold, confident steps. "How are you doing, my dear?"

She glanced at Jim and could tell he wasn't happy to see Roman or to hear his casual address. "I'm all right," she said, turning her attention back to her guest.

"I'm glad to hear that. I know your uncle's death was a terrible shock."

In spite of her resolve not to cry anymore, tears pooled in her eyes. She studied Roman's fancy alligator-skin boots for a moment until she regained her composure. He reached out, using his index finger to lift her chin.

"I came to see if you still want to have dinner with me this weekend."

Sasha felt as if she'd been slapped. Her uncle was barely buried, and Roman was concerned about their dinner engagement?

"I'm sorry, but I'm still mourning my uncle. I'm afraid I must decline."

Roman glanced at Jim, his brows dipping down, lips pursed. "Is it because of him that you won't dine with me?"

"What?" Sasha blinked.

"Every time I see you you're with him. Is there something going on between the two of you?" He glared at her with black, beady eyes.

Sasha felt suddenly weak. How could Roman turn on her so quickly? Was he truly jealous?

Jim stepped forward, his arms crossed. "I think you'd better leave."

"I don't take orders from hired hands." Though Roman huffed, he backed up a step when Jim moved closer.

Jim clenched his fist, and Sasha knew she needed to intervene. "Please, Roman, this isn't the time. I've just buried my uncle. I can't think about having dinner with you now."

He hiked up his chin when Jim sidled up beside her. "Maybe you just prefer white men to being with your own kind."

Sasha gasped. Jim rushed forward and shoved Roman against his horse.

"It's time you left."

The spooked horse jerked its head and sidestepped, causing Roman to fumble for his footing. Roman glared at Jim as he regained his balance. Then anger twisted his handsome features. He mounted his horse and yanked on the reins, making the mare squeal. After a final glare, he kicked the poor beast in the side, urging it into a run.

seventeen

Sasha rinsed the last plate from breakfast and dried it with a towel, then set it in the cabinet. She shut the door and ran her hand over the smooth wood. Such a lovely home. . .but how much longer would she live here?

If they didn't find her uncle's will, she might be on her way back to New York in another week.

Even if she wanted to continue living here, could she do so without her uncle? She'd decorated the home for him, and not having him here to enjoy it stole her pleasure in the house. Tears stung her eyes, and she swiped the back of her hand across them.

The sound of voices outside lured her to the back door. She pushed opened the screen and stepped out into the warm sunshine, the air nearly stealing her breath. With New York being so much cooler, she'd not yet gotten used to the heat here. Using her hand, she fanned her face and looked to see who had arrived. Her heart jolted when she saw Mary and Rita. This was the day they were to begin working, and she'd completely forgotten. Should she tell the women they no longer had employment?

Mary glanced up from talking with Jim, her eyes dancing with excitement. "This is a fine house you have here. I'm delighted to be able to take care of it."

Sasha winced and glanced at Jim, who gave a slight shrug. She couldn't disappoint these women. Even if they only worked for a week, they'd probably make more money than they normally would in a month. She looked past Mary and Rita to see an adolescent boy leading a pitiful donkey pulling a cart. Behind him, an older girl held a toddler boy, and Mary's two children squirmed around the girl's skirt.

"That's Rita's boy, Timmy. He borrowed a neighbor's cart and brung our tents. You said we could set them up here until our room is done. It's a far piece to walk every day."

Sasha smiled, hoping to relieve Mary's concern. "Oh, yes, that would be fine. Why don't you have Timmy set your tents up over there?" She pointed to a bare area behind the house that was sheltered by a large oak tree.

The thin woman stepped forward and curtsied. "I'm Rita Lancaster, ma'am. I'll be doing the cooking for ya. I thank ya for the job." Her pale cheeks turned a rosy shade.

Sasha smiled, thinking Rita could stand to eat a few solid meals. "It's a pleasure to meet you, Mrs. Lancaster. This is Jim Conners." She waved her hand at him. "He's the one who built this lovely house, and he helps with other things, too. I'm sure if you ever need his assistance he'd be happy to help out."

The women turned toward Jim, and he tipped his hat. "Nice to make your acquaintance."

Both women smiled and nodded, then turned back to Sasha.

Mary pointed to the children behind the cart. "That there's my two children, Leah and Phillip, and Rita's girl, Angie, and little Christopher. Angie's gonna watch over the young'uns while we work."

Sasha nodded a greeting at the children, feeling a tingle of apprehension snake down her spine. She'd never been around children much.

"What would you like for us to do first, ma'am?" Mary asked.

"Why don't you go ahead and take today to get settled?"

A worried look passed between Mary and Rita. "We'd just as soon get to work, if that's all right with you. Timmy can set up the tents, and Angie and the children can unpack our belongings."

Timmy guided the donkey over to the spot Sasha had indicated and started unloading. Jim crossed the yard and helped him lift the tents from the cart.

"The children are welcome to play, but it might be a good idea if they stay out of the barn. Oh, and there's a pond that the little ones will need to steer clear of." Sasha hoped she wasn't being too bossy, but she didn't want the youngsters to get hurt.

Mary and Rita nodded and glanced at Angie, who also tipped her head in agreement.

"All right then"—Sasha clapped her hands—"I guess we should all get busy."

The women followed her into the house, and she gave them a tour, appreciating their oohs and aahs at her decorating talents. Sasha enjoyed sharing the house with the women and hoped deep within that they all could become friends.

"I should probably get started in the kitchen, iffen we're to have dinner by noon." At Sasha's nod, Rita busied herself in the kitchen.

Sasha left Mary upstairs to straighten Dewey's room and to pack up his clothing so Timmy could take it back to Rag Town and distribute the items when he returned the cart and donkey.

Sasha hurried down the steps. They had to locate Dewey's will. It was no longer just her well-being that depended on finding it, but Mary's, Rita's, and the children's, as well.

❧

Sasha slammed shut the tack room door, sending a cloud of

dust and hay particles dancing on the dappled light of the barn. Her pretty mouth sagged with disappointment, and Jim wanted nothing more than to kiss away all her problems. But that would be no solution at all, because after kissing her, the problems would still be there.

"I don't know where else to look." Leaning against the barn, she crossed her arms over her chest. "What are we going to do?"

Jim shook his head. "I don't know. There's still the cabin. The remains should be cool enough by now that I can sift through them."

Sasha pushed away from the wall. "I can help."

He took a stance, knowing she'd object, but he didn't want her long skirts anywhere near those ashes, just in case some were still smoldering. "You'd better go back to the house and check on your workers."

"I trust them to work without me watching over them."

Jim moved closer. "That's not the point. Rita is probably fine in the kitchen, but Mary may not know what you want her to do."

"Oh. I hadn't thought of that. I guess I could have her wash Uncle Dewey's bedding." Her shoulders sagged, like she bore an ox yoke all by herself.

He brushed his hand over her cheek, wishing he could take away her troubles just like the streak of dirt he wiped off her face. "We'll get through this. I can't believe God would bring you here only to see you lose your uncle and your home."

Her lower lip trembled, and her eyes shimmered with unshed tears. "Oh, Jim, I miss him so much. I barely had a chance to get to know him before he was taken away."

"I know, I know." He cupped her face in his hands. "You're not in this alone. I'm here, and God's still here, even if it doesn't always seem that way."

"Why would God allow hoodlums to kill a sweet man like my uncle?"

Jim shook his head. He'd asked the same thing, but there was no answer for such a question. "I don't know, but I do know that God is still in control—and we have to believe that. All right?"

Sasha's lips quivered again, but she nodded.

"That's my girl."

Her mouth turned up in a shy smile. "Well. . .I guess I need to get back to the house. I probably should make a trip into town and stock up on some more food and supplies since we have so many mouths to feed now."

"Want me to hitch up the wagon?"

"That would be very nice of you." She beamed a pleased smile, and it took every ounce of self-control not to pull her into his arms and kiss her. But this wasn't the time. He needed to guard his heart, because if Sasha returned to New York, he feared it might just crack in two.

Down at the cabin, Jim used a rake and sifted through the dirt and ashes for an hour. Having moved his belongings into the cabin the day before the fire, he'd lost everything except his tent, which he had stowed in the barn. Thankfully, his money was safe in the Keaton bank.

He sighed in frustration. Nothing remained from the fire except a tin cup and the cast iron skillet. He threw the rake to the ground, stirring up a cloud of ash, and shoved his hands in his back pockets. This was just a waste of time.

Glancing heavenward, he watched some clouds, gray with moisture, drift along, threatening to drop their precious cargo any minute. He needed to finish sorting through this mess before that happened, or he'd look like he'd been tarred and feathered with ash.

He glanced heavenward again. "Father God, I need some help here. I'm at a loss as to what to do. If we don't find that will, Sasha will lose everything. I can't believe Dewey would build that big house, even though he never knew if Sasha and her mother would ever visit, only to leave it to the town. I know he'd want Sasha to have his property, even if she'd never come here. Dewey would have wanted to keep his land in the family. Help us find that will, Lord. And help me be the encouragement Sasha needs.

"Lord, help me also to come to grips with being part Indian. I don't like to think I'm prejudiced, but I must be. You formed me before I was born. As Your Word says, help me to be the man You want me to be and accept my heritage. It doesn't change who I am."

He heaved a sigh, feeling a weight lift off his shoulders. Stepping forward to retrieve the rake, his foot collided with something hard. The dull thunk indicated a container of some sort. With renewed fervor, he dropped to the ground and dug through the ashes. A blackened box began to take shape, and his hopes soared like an eagle taking flight.

Grabbing the box, he shook it free of the ashes, then he stood and carried it over to the chopping block. Sitting down, Jim held his breath. This had to be it. He used his knife to pry open the latch, misshapen from the heat of the fire. It clinked off and flipped to the ground.

Jim's heart felt like a bronc trying to bust out of a chute. "Please, Lord."

With a shaking hand, he lifted the lid and saw a leather pouch smelling strongly of smoke. He loosened the tie and pulled out a roll of papers. His heart quickened even more as he unrolled the thick sheaf.

The will!

His gaze swiftly scanned the papers, which left everything Dewey owned to Sasha, except for his saddle horse and five thousand dollars, which he left to Jim.

He gasped. That much money was far more than he needed to buy his land. He could even build a nice house and furnish it—not fancy like Dewey's—but simple, like a farmer needed. He glanced at the date and the attorney's signature. This will was dated just a week before Dewey's death, and Jim knew in his heart that it was the most current version.

He jumped up, running for the house. He had to tell Sasha that her home was safe.

eighteen

Anxious to get to town and back, Sasha gave Mary a list of things to do, then headed for the barn. She'd told Rita not to worry about her being back in time for dinner, but that she'd be looking forward to their first supper together. She hoped it didn't hurt Rita's feelings that she wasn't there for the first meal that the woman was making, but the sky was clouding up. Sasha wanted to get the food supplies home before it rained, or she might have to wait days for the road to dry out. Besides, she needed something to keep her mind occupied other than her troubles. She'd seen Jim digging through the ashes, but he'd been so deep in thought, she didn't think he even saw her leave.

As she walked into the mercantile an hour later, all manner of scents assailed her, from pungent spices to pickles to leather goods. The store owner glanced past the customer she was helping and flashed a smile.

"Be with you in a few minutes."

Sasha nodded and checked her list. Rita would need lots more sugar to cook up goodies for the children. She couldn't help smiling, knowing how much Jim would also enjoy the treats. That man had an appetite bigger than the whole state of New York, not that anyone would notice with his lean, muscular form.

Shaking her head, she pulled her thoughts away from Jim and studied her list. She'd need more flour, canned goods, and fresh vegetables, but she also needed to be frugal. If they didn't find the will, then her little family would be scattered in three different directions. But then again, she could send any leftover food back with Mary and Rita if things turned out for the worst. Making a mental note to up the quantities, she turned back to the counter.

Wilma Plunkett wiped her plump hands on her apron. "Now, how can I help you?"

Sasha borrowed a stubby pencil, changed the amounts, added several items, and then handed the long list back to Mrs. Plunkett. The woman's eyes widened.

"I sure hope you aren't in a hurry. It might take a while to gather up all of this. Plus, my Henry will have to load it, and he's down at the livery just now."

"My wagon is right outside, so he can load it whenever he's ready." Sasha's stomach suddenly rumbled, and she glanced at the storekeeper, hoping the woman didn't hear. "Perhaps I'll go eat something at the diner while I wait."

Mrs. Plunkett flashed a knowing smile. "Sounds like that might be a good idea."

They shared a laugh, and Sasha walked back outside, peeking up at the sky. The clouds were dispersing and looked less threatening than before. Just maybe she'd get home without getting wet.

As she entered the diner, it took a moment for her eyes to adjust to the dimmer lighting. Fragrant scents tickled her nose, and the hum of conversation mixed with the clinking of silverware. She noticed an empty table in the corner and headed for it, but just before she reached her destination, a man stood up, blocking her path.

Roman Loftus.

Sasha scowled, remembering their last encounter.

He met her glare with one of complete humbleness. "I owe

you an apology, Miss Di Carlo."

She wanted to skirt around him or run back out the door but couldn't in the face of his surprising meekness.

"I acted dreadfully the other day. I make no excuses for my ridiculous behavior." His hands drifted open in a stance of surrender. "Please accept my humble apology by joining me for dinner."

She glanced at his table and saw that he hadn't yet received his meal. Never one to hold a grudge—even on an occasion when she sometimes wanted to—she smiled at him. "All right, Mr. Loftus, I'll dine with you—and apology accepted."

In spite of her initial reservations, she enjoyed the meal, although Roman monopolized the conversation talking about his father's oil business. Much to her disappointment, no mention was made of the men whom she'd overheard talking about cheating Indians. Taking Roman's proffered arm, she allowed him to escort her back to the store once they'd finished eating.

Just outside the door, he tugged her to a stop. "I wonder if you'd consider having dinner with me this Friday evening."

Sasha shook her head. In her heart, she knew there was no future for the two of them, and it irked her that he was so persistent, considering she'd just lost her uncle and was still mourning him. And for all she knew, she might well be packing to leave by Friday. "I don't think that's a good idea in light of all that's going on right now."

Roman pursed his lips and stepped sideways to allow two older women to pass. He looked around, then back at her. "Come with me, please. There's something I want to talk to you about."

In spite of her reservations, she followed him into the alley. Her heart picked up its pace, but she felt perfectly safe with so many people walking past on the nearby boardwalks. Roman had never threatened her. His frustration had always been directed at Jim. Roman shoved his hands into the pockets of his fine trousers and paced a few feet away and back.

"This isn't at all how I'd planned this." He glanced at Sasha, with a look of apology.

"Whatever it is, please just say it. I need to be getting back home."

He sighed and stopped in front of her. She took a half step backward to put some space between them.

"All right. I know your uncle's death was a shock—and then finding out that he left his property to the town. . .well, it must have felt like a kick in the teeth. I guess you're planning to go back to New York soon."

She saw the question in his dark eyes but didn't understand where he was going with his little speech. "I've not yet given up hope of finding my uncle's will. I believe it will prove differently than what you've said."

He pursed his lips and shook his head. "If the will was around, you'd have found it by now. In another week, you'll be evicted. I don't want you to go back to New York, Sasha."

She opened her mouth to comment, but when he reached for her hand, she slammed her lips together. Her mind raced, trying to imagine what he wanted.

"What I'm trying to say is. . .I want to marry you." Looking a bit embarrassed, he lifted his derby hat and ran his fingers through his straight, black hair. "You'll need a place to live and someone to take care of you. I want to be that person."

Sasha blinked, numb from his surprising proposal. She noticed he didn't ask her to marry him, but simply told her he wanted to. Her mind swarmed with excuses, but she didn't want to seem coldhearted.

"I thank you for your kind offer, but I'm afraid I'm not in a position to marry right now. There are too many loose ends that need to be tied up."

Roman's congenial look shifted to one of displeasure. It was obvious he hadn't expected her to turn him down. Most of Keaton's single women would have considered him the catch of the town, but she saw past his fine looks and into his murky heart. She suspected that by marrying her, he hoped to somehow gain control of Dewey's property, but with it going to the town, she failed to see how that was possible.

"I could help you, if you'd let me." His eyes pleaded with her to accept his offer.

"Thank you, but no. I can't marry you." She pivoted and rushed out of the alley back into the mercantile, praying he wouldn't follow. She'd had her fill of Roman Loftus and only wanted to get her supplies and leave town.

Mr. Plunkett was almost done loading the wagon. The man was shorter than his wife but muscled from years of hauling supplies. As she waited for Mrs. Plunkett to finish with her customer, she watched Roman stalk off. Sasha longed to be married and settled, but Roman wasn't the man she envisioned herself with.

It was Jim. He was the one who made her heart flutter. He was a man to look up to—a kind, caring man.

Why couldn't he show an interest in her like Roman had? Was a simple kiss all he wanted from her?

☙

Jim tightened the cinch and stepped up into the saddle. His horse snorted and fidgeted, anxious to be off. Jim hadn't wanted to stop and eat dinner, because he was in a hurry to tell Sasha the good news, but he'd gone to the house looking for her and found dinner ready. Not wanting to disappoint Rita, he'd wolfed down her delicious stew and fresh biscuits. He adored Sasha, but his belly sure was glad she'd hired Rita to do the cooking. He swatted his horse with the ends of the reins and clicked out the side of his mouth. His mount took off at a fast clip.

As he rounded the third bend in the road, he saw Sasha and the wagon coming over the hill.

"He'yah!" Jim nudged his horse into a gallop, eating up the distance between him and the wagon. His stomach churned with eager anticipation at the prospect of Sasha's surprised expression.

At the bottom of the hill, Sasha stopped the wagon and stood up with her hand blocking the sun from her eyes. He could tell she was worried. As he pulled alongside the wagon, he yanked his horse to a quick stop and jumped off.

"What's wrong? Has someone been hurt?" Sasha started to climb down, but he lifted up his arms and hoisted her to the ground.

He couldn't quit grinning. "I found it! I found the will!" His hands on her upper arms tightened.

Sasha's concern instantly changed to joy, and she leaned forward, hugging him. "Oh, that's wonderful! Where did you find it?"

He wrapped his arms around her and held her close. "At the cabin. I found a box that must have been under the floorboards. It was charred but still intact." Leaning back, he looked her in the eye. "Your uncle left almost everything to you and nothing to the town."

Astonishment widened her eyes. "Truly?"

"Yes. There was a new amendment to the will dated a week before Dewey died."

"Oh, I'm so relieved. I wanted so badly to stay here and not go back to New York. Everything I love is here."

Jim studied her face until her cheeks turned a dark red.

More than ever, he wanted Sasha to marry him, but now, they were even further apart. She was a wealthy woman. And yes, he had the money Dewey had left him—or would soon—and the money in the bank, but it didn't come close to Sasha's wealth. If he confessed his love now, she'd just think he was after her property, like Roman Loftus. His joy gone, he stepped back.

"What's wrong?"

He shrugged. "Nothing. I'm just relieved we found the will."

"Where is it?"

"Safe. I hid it in the place I used to hide my money before I started putting it in the bank."

"Good." Sasha glanced over her shoulder at the wagon. "I guess we'd better get this food home. Then what should we do about the will since the attorney is gone?"

"I'll go talk to the sheriff and see what he thinks." He lifted her back into the wagon, amazed at her trust in him. She didn't pressure him about where the will was but simply trusted him to take care of it. His chest swelled a bit.

Jim picked his horse's reins. "You were gone quite a while. What took so long?"

Sasha glanced down at him, her lips pressed together as if she didn't want to tell him. "Mrs. Plunkett said it would take some time to gather up all my supplies, so since I missed dinner, I ate at the diner."

Jim nodded and mounted his horse.

"I. . .uh. . .ate with Roman Loftus."

Feeling as if he'd been shot with a renegade arrow, he spun his mount around to face her.

"Sasha! How could you—after the way he treated us the other day!" He clenched his jaw, just thinking about Sasha being in that scoundrel's company. Couldn't she see Loftus was a wolf in sheep's clothing?

Jiggling the reins, she made a kissing smack, which set the horses in motion. The wagon groaned as if in pain and creaked forward. "I didn't *plan* to eat with him. He was just there—and so remorseful that it seemed cruel not to accept his apology."

"I don't understand why you can't see him for who he is."

Sasha glared at him. "I realize he's rather shallow, but that doesn't mean we shouldn't treat him as nice as the next person."

"You're far too sweet and naïve." Jim reached over and pulled on the reins, stopping the wagon. The two horses snorted and pawed the ground. "Loftus only wants to get control of your uncle's property—and he's not above using you to do so."

"You're just jealous." She sat back and crossed her arms, not mentioning that she'd thought the very same thing about Roman just a short while ago. Why did they have to argue about him? She'd never planned to accept his dinner invitation again.

Jim's stormy black eyes looked as if they would spit forth lightning bolts any second. "Along with your uncle's will was Kizzie Arbuckle's land deed and her oil lease." He looked at her long and hard. "The lease papers were signed by Roman Loftus—*president* of Chamber Oil."

Sasha blinked, confusion numbing her mind. "But how could that be? Roman never even mentioned Chamber Oil."

Jim's gaze softened. "Maybe that's because he *owns* it. He's been stringing you along all this time."

She gasped. Wave after wave of shock slapped at her. "He tricked me."

Jim's horse danced around, and he turned his mount back to face her. "Loftus only wanted the land so Chamber Oil could drill and make him richer. It wasn't about you, Sasha; it was always about the land."

nineteen

Sasha unloaded a couple of canned food items from the crate and handed one to Leah and the other to Philip. The children were having a grand time running the cans over to the pantry, handing them to Rita, and skipping back. Their sweet smiles softened her aching heart.

She'd always been so careful to guard her heart. Now Jim was upset with her, and her heart hurt because of it.

She had also thought Roman had become a friend, even though his temper got the best of him at times, but she'd seen his signature with her own eyes. Roman Loftus was president of Chamber Oil—a company he'd never even mentioned to her. He lied and tried to woo her to get at her uncle's property. Those three men who'd pestered her uncle probably worked for him.

But how could he, being full-blooded Creek, be callous enough to cheat his own people—and maybe even his own family?

She should have known by the way Roman always talked about his father's company whenever she tried to talk about Chamber Oil. He was deftly deflecting her to a different subject. How could she have been so stupid?

She slammed the can onto the counter, making Leah jump. The girl stared at her with wide blue eyes.

"Sorry, sweetie. I was just thinking about something that upset me."

Leah smiled and reached for the can before her brother

could get it, then she darted back toward the pantry. Philip stared up at her with sparkling eyes, holding his palm out. Sasha handed him the final two cans, and his eyes widened along with his smile.

"She gived me two of dem," he said, trotting back to the pantry, carefully carrying his bounty.

Sasha lugged the empty crate outside, passing Jim as he carried in a twenty-five pound sack of flour. His warm smile made her insides tingle. Perhaps he wasn't so upset, after all.

At least she'd done the right thing upping her food quantities and wouldn't have to return to the mercantile for more supplies for a while and chance running into Roman again. She set the crate next to the others and wandered down the hill toward the pond.

At the water's edge, she tossed in a pebble and watched the ripples it made. A mother duck swam on the far side of the pond with her ducklings, snapping up an unsuspecting insect every so often. Sasha swatted at a mosquito that hummed past her ear.

What was her mother doing now? Did she miss her?

Roman Loftus's character was so similar to her mother's that it surprised her that she hadn't noticed before now. Her mother only cared about fame and fortune, even walking away from her only child when given the choice between Sasha and a wealthy man.

Sasha had tried all her life to be good enough to earn her mother's love, but she'd never succeeded. Until she met Dewey, she'd never known what unconditional love was. In the short time she'd known him, Dewey had loved her that way, but he'd said that God was the only One who could truly give her the security she longed for.

Tears pooled in her eyes and burned her throat. She'd had such high hopes for a new life here in Indian Territory, but the one person who'd truly loved her was dead. Could she live in the big house alone? Did she even want to?

For so long, she'd thought having family, a home, and setting down roots would fill the empty spot inside her. Now she had a home and plenty of money, but that emptiness was still there.

From a distance, she heard the children's laughter, and hope flickered anew. At least she was helping a couple of the widows and their families. Maybe she could somehow figure out a way to help the others. She lifted her gaze toward the heavens. *God, if You're truly up there and care about people, show me what to do with all that I've been given.*

⁂

Jim hated to disturb Sasha, but he needed to apologize. She looked so lonely there standing by the pond. His boot snapped a twig, and Sasha spun around, staring at him with damp eyes. He walked toward her, noticing she looked as melancholy as he felt. He came to a stop several feet away and studied the ground. Finally, he looked at her. "I'm sorry for getting upset about you eating with Loftus."

She waved her hand in the air. "No, you were right, but I didn't know everything you knew at the time. I won't ever have anything to do with Roman Loftus again if I can help it."

"Well. . .for what it's worth, I'm sorry. I know you cared about him."

Sasha shook her head, but her tears told Jim that she cared more for Loftus than he'd thought. He felt his own dreams die a little more. She leaned forward, crying into her hands, and he couldn't help pulling her to his chest. He'd hold her one last time, build her cabins, then ride out as soon as things were settled and she had control of her land.

Maybe if he worked hard enough on the land he wanted to buy in the Oklahoma Territory, he could forget her. Forget how her eyes twinkled before she teased him. Forget her long lashes clustered together from the tears she'd shed. He was a simple farmer and carpenter. How could he compete with the likes of wealthy oilmen?

Sasha finally had the home she'd craved for so long. He couldn't ask her to give that up.

He rested his head on her silky, rose-scented hair and held her tightly, wanting to remember this moment with her in his arms and the sun glistening on the pond. A light breeze lifted the rebellious strands of Sasha's hair that had escaped her long braid, and he smoothed them down. All too soon, she sniffed and pulled back.

"I didn't care for Roman like you think. He was a friend— of sorts. A while back, I overhead some oilmen talking about cheating Indians. I needed his help to try to find the men responsible." Her thin brows dipped down, and she uttered an unlady-like snort. "I was asking help of the very man responsible. How could I have been so naïve?"

She stared up at him as if she expected a response, but all he could focus on was that she didn't care for Loftus. "You really didn't care about him?"

"What?" She blinked, then her confused expression softened. "Well, yes, as a friend. He could be quite charming, but I never thought of him as anything more. Why?"

A mallard near the pond flapped its wings and took flight, just like Jim's heart. He couldn't help smiling as he stared down at Sasha. He loved her sweet innocence. Her kindheartedness, and her truthfulness. There wasn't a deceitful bone in her body.

"Sasha, do you think you could ever care for *me*?" The question was tough to voice, but he had to know.

She opened her mouth to respond, but he laid his fingers across her velvety lips. "Don't answer that yet. There's something I need to tell you first. All my life, I thought my family was part French. But I recently got a letter from my uncle.

He told me about a long-held family secret—my great-grandmother, it turns out, was a full-blooded Creek Indian."

Sasha's eyes widened as surprise engulfed her face. She blinked several times. Then her lips curved up in a smile that sent a vibrant chord of hope strumming through his being. She laid her hand against his cheek, and he leaned into it.

"I already care about you, Jim. It doesn't matter a whit to me if you're Indian or white. I care about the kind, sensitive man you are."

He kissed her then—taking his time, raining gentle kisses on her mouth, then trailing up to her eyes and ears. Holding her tight, he knew she was the woman for him. If only—

Suddenly, he stopped and pulled back, his breath coming fast. As much as he loved Sasha, even if she cared for him, he couldn't have her—unless she gave her heart to God.

In spite of his feelings for her, he couldn't—no, wouldn't—make that compromise, even if it meant riding away and never seeing her again.

Sasha gave him a shy but confused smile and stepped back. "I suppose I should go help Mary and Rita finish putting the food away."

She darted around him, and he let her go.

This time.

He had a lot of praying to do. Surely God wouldn't allow him to love Sasha so deeply if He hadn't meant for them to be together. Sasha had been very open to Dewey's Bible teaching, and she'd asked them both plenty of questions. He'd pray and nurture her, and soon—he felt it in his heart—she would give her life over to God.

And then maybe they could have a future together.

But if not, Sasha would be safe in the arms of his heavenly Father.

twenty

Sasha drove the buggy the final half mile to the barn. One day they'd have a nice, new one, but for now, Dewey's old barn near the burned-out cabin sufficed. Today had been a good day.

She smiled, knowing Jim had shown the will to the sheriff yesterday, and he had said that nothing would be done until the town attorney returned. The sheriff also said he would lean on the three men who'd been pestering Dewey to see if they had anything to do with his death or were connected to Chamber Oil. If only they could discover who had killed her uncle and make them pay the price, then everything would be wonderful.

The light breeze lifted the scarf of her Gypsy costume and threatened to steal it away. Holding the reins with one hand, she grabbed her scarf with her free hand. She tucked it back around her face and pulled on the reins so the horse would slow. The anxious animal resisted, knowing the barn was just around the corner. But she had to be cautious. Jim and Timmy were supposed to be out checking the cattle today, but they could always return early.

With nobody in sight, she urged the buggy into the clearing beside the barn, stopped, and set the brake. As she climbed down, she heard Jim's voice in the stable. Her heart jumped almost up to her throat, and she darted behind the building, thankful to find the back doors closed.

Picking up her skirts, she hurried down to the creek and followed it back to the main house. By staying off the road, maybe she wouldn't be seen. Her change of clothes was hidden in the barn, but if she could get into the house without being noticed, then she could dress in her room.

But that was a big "if" with so many people around the house now.

She hated this deception, but it was for a good reason. Wasn't it?

If she hadn't wanted to help the other widows by taking some clothing to them, she didn't think she would have used her costume again. Here, in Indian Territory, she could be herself and no longer needed a costume to hide behind. Still, the poor but proud widows seemed more willing to accept an old beggar woman's help than a wealthy landowner's, even if she was the same person on the inside.

She jolted to a stop at the sound of children's voices as Rita and all the kids headed her way. Sasha's heart felt as if it would beat clear out of her chest. She ducked down, hiding behind a thick cluster of bushes. Thankfully the dark colors of her clothing blended with the landscape.

"Can we really swim?" Leah asked, her high-pitched voice carrying a bit of awe.

"Yes, but you must stay in the shallow water." Dried leaves left over from last winter crunched as Rita passed her carrying several thin, frayed towels.

Sasha made a mental note to purchase new ones for the cabins. The younger children skipped past, followed by Timmy and Angie.

Timmy snorted and leaned close to the adolescent girl. "Swim—yeah. They don't know this is just Mom's attempt at getting them clean before supper."

Angie giggled and nodded her head. "I don't mind though. As hot as it's been, the water. . ." Her voice faded as she moved out of hearing distance.

A bead of sweat trickled down Sasha's back, making her wish she could join them in the cool water. She took a final look around and darted to the back of the house, then stopped to listen. Jim had been in the barn, probably talking to his horse. All the children were with Rita, so that left only Mary.

Taking a deep breath, she dashed in the back door and past the kitchen. Mary was most likely upstairs. As she passed the parlor, she heard a bang and jumped.

"Hey there, what are you doing in here? Stop! Now!"

Sasha darted for the stairs, not sure what to do, but Mary snagged hold of her skirt. "I don't want to hurt you, but you don't belong in here. If it's food you want, you only have to ask."

Sasha fought to get away, but Mary yanked on her scarf, and Sasha's mass of hair tumbled down around her shoulders.

Mary gasped and turned Sasha around. "Ma'am?" Her brows dipped.

Sasha heaved a sigh. "Yes, Mary, it's me."

With her hands on her cheeks, Mary stepped back. "I'm sorry for scolding you. . .but why are you dressed like that?" Utter shock replaced her normally pleasant features. "Were you the old woman who brought me that fabric?"

Sasha saw confusion in Mary's eyes and stared at the floor. She nodded.

"But why?"

She looked at her friend. "I didn't think you'd accept help from a wealthy woman, and I wanted so badly to help you. Uncle Dewey told me that sometimes the rich women in town simply wore a dress once or twice and tossed it in the refuse pile afterwards. In New York, the wealthy often gave their clothing to their employees or shelters for the poor. I couldn't stand perfectly good clothing going to waste when you had such a need." She was rambling, she knew, but the pain in Mary's eyes cut her to the quick.

"I suppose I owe you an apology." Mary gave her a weak smile. "We have so little in Rag Town that our pride is something we cling to. Pride in poverty, maybe. I'm sorry that I was so proud that you felt you had to use a disguise to help me. Please forgive me."

Stunned, Sasha stared at Mary. The mantle clock in the parlor ticked a steady beat that matched the rhythm of her heart. Mary was asking Sasha's forgiveness when she'd done nothing wrong. "I'm the one who needs forgiveness. I didn't mean to trick you—only to help."

"We all need God's forgiveness—and other people's help at times."

Sasha blurted out, "But how do I get God's forgiveness?" She had never wanted anything so badly in her life.

Mary smiled. "Do you believe Jesus is God's only Son? And that He died for your sins?"

"Yes, I do." Sasha nodded.

Mary took her hand. "Then tell that to God and ask Him to forgive your sins. It's that simple."

She closed her eyes and did as Mary said, then Mary prayed for her and they hugged. Sasha stepped back, feeling whole for the first time in her life. Jim would be so happy to hear she gave her heart to God.

The back door banged shut. "Mary, have you seen Sasha? The buggy's at the barn, but I can't find—"

Sasha sensed the moment Jim noticed her. He tugged off his hat and stepped closer. His smile suddenly dropped and his brow crinkled as he took her in from head to toe.

"Sasha?"

❧

"Yes, it's me." Sasha's voice sounded hollow.

"*You're* the Gypsy woman? It was you all the time?"

She nodded and stood perfectly still. Mary patted her arm, then slipped away, leaving them alone.

"Why?" Jim couldn't voice everything he felt. Betrayed, deceived, lied to—just like his father had done all his life.

"It's complicated, but in New York, dressing like this was the only way I could go out on the streets alone. There were times I had to get away from the theater, and this is how I did it. Nobody bothers an old woman." Sasha's gaze begged him to understand.

"I took a beating for you. Why didn't you tell me?"

Her shoulders lifted in a pitiful shrug. "I wanted to, but after you got beat up, I was. . .afraid to tell you."

Jim had never known such deep emotional pain. "I trusted you. Loved you. But you're a liar, just like my ol' man." He slammed on his hat, turned, and strode outside, savoring the loud bang the screen door made.

"You should forgive Miss Sasha. Her intentions were good."

He halted at Mary's soft voice, his boots slinging pebbles spiraling across the yard. "She deceived me."

"She had a good reason to dress as she did. Sasha didn't mean to hurt you, Mr. Conners." Mary glanced down at her folded hands, then peeked at him. "You'll be happy to know she just gave her heart to God."

Jim closed his eyes. He'd prayed for this. Ought to be joyous about it. But there was nothing on God's earth that he despised worse than a deceiver. He shook his head and stalked away.

Half an hour later, Jim felt only marginally better. He'd ridden out to the fields and checked on the cattle, but he had ended up at the remains of Dewey's cabin, wishing his old friend were there to offer advice. He'd been ready to pack up his meager belongings and head home, but something had stopped him.

One thing he'd learned from Sasha was the value of family. At one time, he'd had to get away from his, but now he ached to see them. His sister, Katie, and her young son. His aunt and uncle. Even their rowdy kids. A smile tugged at his lips. Yeah, he actually missed his family. That was something.

Finally, weak from all the emotions that had roiled through him, Jim look at the endless blue sky. "What do I do, Lord? You know how hard I've prayed for Sasha to give her heart to You, and now she has. But You also know how much I hate a fraud—a deceiver. I fought twice for Sasha and didn't even know it was her.

"Was that why You brought us together? So I could guide her toward You?

"I never wanted a woman in my life until I met her. But now everything's changed."

His horse pawed the ground, restless to move. Jim dismounted and dropped to his knees. "Show me what to do, Lord. Help me to forgive Sasha and trust again. And help me to forgive my father."

❧

With her clothes changed and makeup removed, Sasha still felt awful. She couldn't get Jim's stricken expression out of her mind. He'd been her one true friend, and she'd shattered his view of her.

How could she make amends?

She had to find him.

Grabbing her wadded-up costume, she hurried downstairs. Rita had banked the fire in the stove until she needed it for dinner. Sasha tossed her disguise into the ashes, poked the garments with a stick, and watched them ignite.

As she stepped outside, Mary was pacing back and forth

with her hands folded under her chin. She glanced up, an apologetic look on her thin face. "I tried to stop him, but he was just so angry."

"I'll find him. I have to make him understand."

Mary nodded. "I'll keep praying. God will work things out."

"I sure hope so." Sasha lifted her skirts and jogged down the hill past the pond. She didn't know why, but she felt a pull to Dewey's cabin. It was the first place where she'd found true happiness. Where she was valued for what she was on the inside and not what she looked like or who her mother was.

The memory of the pain in Jim's eyes threatened to knock her to her knees. Besides Dewey, he'd been the only person ever to stand by her. To protect her. To be her friend. Somehow, she *had* to salvage their friendship. She didn't think she could live without it.

She loved him, deep in her heart, like she'd never loved anyone else before. This love was different from what she'd felt for her uncle, and it amazed her.

As she neared the rubble that had been her uncle's home, she skidded to a halt. Jim knelt in the ashes of the cabin with his hands over his face, his horse grazing nearby. Her whole body quivered with the need to make things right. To see him smile again.

Help me, Lord.

જ

Jim felt as if he were two men wrestling. The one man despised Sasha for her deception while the other loved her and wanted to make a life with her. He hated feeling weak and at odds with himself. The conflict was tearing him apart.

He wanted to stay mad. He wanted to forgive her.

The scripture verse where Peter asked how many times he should forgive his brother came to mind.

"Seven?" Peter had asked.

But Jesus had responded, "Seven times seventy."

A smile tugged at his lips. As a boy he'd told his uncle that if he forgave Katie four hundred ninety times, then he wouldn't ever have to forgive her again. He'd followed his ornery sister around saying, "I forgive you," so many times he'd made her fume. In spite of her small size, she'd shoved him down, making him lose count. Too tired to start over, he finally gave up.

Jim heaved a sigh. That wasn't the point Jesus had been trying to make. He needed to forgive Sasha. But how did he do that when she'd shaken him to the very core?

He heard a noise and lowered his hands. Sasha stood there in her pretty dress, looking sad and alone.

She was a gift God was offering to him if he'd only reach out and accept it. But to do so, he had to forgive her—and his father who, by his behavior, had ingrained Jim's hate of deceit into him.

He stood and dusted off his knees and hands. The scent of smoke lingered, mixing with the odor of leather and a faint whiff of Sasha's floral scent.

Forgiveness was a choice. And now he had to make one that could change his life.

Sasha moved closer. "Jim, I'm *so* sorry for not telling you the truth. I only wore my costume for protection and to help the widows. I didn't do it to be sneaky." Sasha's eyes pleaded with him to believe her. "I never meant to deceive you."

He took a step toward her, and she hesitated, then did the same.

One step toward forgiveness.

"It's all right. I understand."

Sasha blinked, looking stunned. Tears flooded her eyes,

then spilled onto her cheeks. "You do?"

He nodded. "I'm sorry for getting so angry. I understand now why you felt you needed the costume. Will you forgive me for getting upset?"

She wheezed a laugh. "Forgive *you*? I'm the one who should be asking that."

Jim closed the distance between them and took her hands. "Then let's just mutually agree to forgive. All right?"

Sasha nodded, smiling in spite of her tears. "Yes, that sounds wonderful."

Jim grinned and dashed his own tears away with the back of his hand. In one quick swoop, he tugged her into his arms and kissed her firmly on the lips. She returned his affection with a fervor that surprised him. Finally, they came up for air.

She reached out and wiped his face. "You've got ashes all across your eyes. You look like a raccoon."

A smile lifted his cheeks. "Then we're a matched pair, because you do, too."

Sasha's giggle blended with the birds chirping and the locusts singing. Oh how he loved her!

And to think, moments ago he'd been willing to give her up because of his hurt and anger. What a loss that would have been.

He tightened his grip and gazed into her eyes, thrilling to the affection he saw there.

"Sasha, will you marry me?"

Stunned, she opened her mouth, then closed it. Slowly, a smile tugged at her cheeks and joy filled her countenance. "Why, yes, Mr. Conners, I believe I'd like that very much."

They laughed and resumed kissing.

As they walked back to the house arm in arm, Jim marveled at the difference an hour could make.

twenty-one

Three weeks later

Sasha jumped aside as Jim's twin cousins darted past her, yelling like banshees. She giggled and shook her head. With his family there, the house buzzed with activity like a bee hive. Jim, along with his brother-in-law, Dusty McIntyre, his uncle Mason, and Mason's oldest son, were busy raising the cabins. Jim's aunt Rebekah and his sister, Katie, had jumped in to help Rita make the wedding cake and food for after the ceremony.

Sasha moved ten-month-old Joey, Dusty and Katie's son, to her left arm. He patted her chest and kicked his chubby legs, begging for another piece of biscuit to gnaw on to ease his sore gums. The cute little boy had stolen Sasha's heart from the start. Deborah, Rebekah's only daughter, wiped her hands on her apron and ambled toward Sasha. "Would you like me to hold him for a while?"

Before Sasha could answer, Joey squealed and dove at Deborah. At thirteen and lovely, she would have young men lining up to court her in a few years. Mason would have to keep his shotgun handy, or some fellow might soon steal Deb's heart.

Sasha walked to the back porch door and looked out. As if he could feel her gaze, Jim glanced up and grinned at her. They stared at one another, making Sasha's heart sing. Oh how she loved him. And tomorrow, they'd be married.

Mason said something, and Jim turned to answer, breaking their connection.

Sasha loved Jim's whole family. They were noisy, the twins especially rambunctious, and could they ever put away the food! But she loved them all. Mason was a kind father figure to Jim. The only loving father he'd ever known. She suspected it wouldn't be too long before Mason held that same position in her heart.

And Rebekah treated her like a daughter and sister both. The kind woman had swooped in and stolen her heart from the beginning. Sasha never knew before how much she'd missed by not having a loving family.

But thank the good Lord, she had one now.

She strolled upstairs to look over her wedding garments to be sure everything was ready for tomorrow. Holding up the lovely gown that Rebekah and Katie had made, she turned to her left and right, surveying herself in the mirror. Would Jim like the dress?

"You'll be a lovely bride." Katie stood in the doorway, leaning against the jamb.

Sasha started. She had been so engrossed in her activities that she hadn't even heard her approach.

"Are you nervous?" Katie asked.

Sasha nodded. "Yes, I suppose all brides are. Weren't you?"

Katie giggled and tucked a strand of her honey blond hair behind her ear. "Truth be told, I couldn't wait to get married. I loved Dusty so much, and we'd gone through some rough times. I'll tell you about them someday." She stepped forward and adjusted a sleeve on Sasha's gown.

"Are you happy with the dress?" Her blue eyes held a trace of apprehension.

"Oh, yes, I love it! You and Rebekah are so talented. I could never have sewn anything like this. In fact, I can barely sew at all. My mother never had time for such domestic things."

Katie laid her hand on Sasha's shoulder. "Aunt Rebekah would be happy to teach you. I would, but Dusty and I live too far away to visit frequently, but we usually get back every couple of months. You'll enjoy living next door to Uncle Mason and Aunt Rebekah. Farming can be lonely."

"I won't mind as long as Jim is there."

Katie chuckled. "I still can't get used to calling him Jim. He's always been Jimmy to me."

Sasha smiled. "I'm sure he would answer to either, especially if you're carrying a tray of sweets.

They shared a laugh, then Katie sobered as she looked around the room. "Are you sure you won't mind leaving this beautiful house? You've done so much work decorating it."

She looked around the room, enjoying the pretty rose theme. "I've learned that a house doesn't make a home. It's the people who live in it. Wherever Jim is, that's my home."

Katie smiled. "You don't know how happy that makes me. We all worried about Jimmy for so long—ever since he fought in the Spanish-American War. He returned home a different man. And he's been troubled for so long."

Katie crossed the room and stood in front of the window, staring out. "None of us wanted him to come here—to Indian Territory. He'd wandered so much that we wanted him home, even if he wasn't the same." She spun around, her long skirt swirling around her legs. "But the old Jimmy has returned, and I have you to thank for that."

Sasha bit back her surprise when Jim's sister hurried over and hugged her. Katie pulled back, looking a tad embarrassed. "So, Aunt Rebekah says you're making this house into a widows' colony."

"Yes. We'll start small and add more cabins if it's successful. Mary has agreed to serve as the overseer, with Rita cooking and assisting her. The first women will move in next week. This room will remain empty so Jim and I can use it when we come back for visits to see how things are going."

"It's a wonderful plan, and I'm sure God will bless it."

They heard a loud cry downstairs, and Katie scurried out the door. "Sounds like Joey's ready to nurse again," she said over her shoulder.

Sasha stepped out onto the balcony and stared at the pond. A tremor of excitement zigzagged through her as she thought about tomorrow. Her wedding day. Tomorrow she'd officially be Jim's wife and part of his family.

&

"I like Sasha—a lot." Mason cupped his hands, dipped them into the creek, and dumped the water over his head.

Jim flashed him a smile. "I rather like her, too."

Mason looked at him, water beading on his eyelashes. "Yeah, I imagine you do. I'm sure glad to see you happy again."

Jim sipped the cool water he'd scooped from the creek, then wiped his nape with his wet hand, finally feeling some relief from the heat. He stood. "Feels good to be happy again. To have my troubles behind me."

Mason slapped him on the shoulder. "I doubt if all your problems are behind you, but whatever the future holds, God will help you."

Jim nodded. "You know, it's odd. When I was seventeen, all I could think of was joining the army and getting away from the farm. I was sick of farming." He ran his hands through his damp hair and stuck his hat back on. "Now I can hardly wait to get back to the Oklahoma Territory, set up a home with Sasha, and start plowing."

Mason chuckled, pulling Jim's gaze to him. "Now you get to *plant* oats instead of sowing wild ones."

Jim smiled, then sobered. "I'm sorry for all the trouble I caused you, Uncle Mason. There were times I resented you raising me instead of my own pa, but I can tell you now, I'm grateful for all you did for Katie and me. You made a huge sacrifice, taking us in after you'd lost your first wife and child."

"We're family." Mason shrugged. "Family cares for family."

"Yeah, that's right."

They stood shoulder to shoulder staring out past the creek, like father and son. Jim knew in his heart Mason had done a far better job as a parent than his own father ever could have. He'd given him a foundation to build on and a faith in God.

"Did you tell Sasha your news yet?" Mason glanced out the corner of his eye at him.

"No. I haven't had a chance. We'll take a walk after supper, and I'll tell her then. She'll be happy to know they caught the men who killed her uncle but disappointed when she learns Roman Loftus was responsible. She liked him for a time." Jim plucked a leaf from a nearby bush and tore it in half, feeling guilty for how jealous he'd been over Sasha's friendship with Loftus. He hoped his news wouldn't affect their wedding. For a fleeting moment, he wondered if he should wait and tell her after the ceremony.

"That Loftus fellow—he's in jail now?"

Jim nodded. "Yep. Guess all that money he accumulated by cheating folks won't be much help to him there."

"Nope."

"Sasha will be happy to learn that the mayor's put together a commission to explore how the Indians were cheated and to see if anything can be done about it now. Most of the oil companies are fair and legitimate, but Chamber Oil sure caused lots of problems. It's nice to know it's out of business."

The dinner bell clanged, and they turned in unison, walking toward the house. Jim whispered a prayer of thanks for all that God had done. A shiver of excitement surged through him, knowing that at this time tomorrow he'd be a married man.

He couldn't wait until he and Sasha had children—a houseful of dark-headed youngsters running around. The thought made him smile, and he thanked God for his heritage and his bride.

❧

Sasha glided down the stairs, knowing her future husband waited. Her heart was so full of joy, she felt sure it would burst. Never in her life had she been so happy. The one shadow on her bright day was that her mother wasn't there. But she and Jim hadn't wanted to wait for her to return from England— even if Cybil would have come. Maybe one day Sasha would see her mother again, but she would be a different woman than the daughter her mother had known.

As she stepped outside, her gaze slid past the small crowd of family and friends and found her beloved. His black eyes beamed his love, and she could tell by his expression that he thought her beautiful. For once, she didn't mind that she was pretty, because it pleased the man she loved.

As she eagerly approached Jim, she thought about the frightened, determined girl who'd left New York nearly four months earlier. That girl no longer existed. God had come into her life and blessed her beyond measure. He had answered her prayers, giving her a wonderful man to marry, the family she'd always longed for, and a place to call home. He'd given her wealth beyond what most people could imagine. But most of all, He'd given her a wealth beyond riches—something for free—His unfailing love.

A Letter To Our Readers

Dear Reader:

In order that we might better contribute to your reading enjoyment, we would appreciate your taking a few minutes to respond to the following questions. We welcome your comments and read each form and letter we receive. When completed, please return to the following:

Fiction Editor
Heartsong Presents
PO Box 719
Uhrichsville, Ohio 44683

1. Did you enjoy reading *A Wealth Beyond Riches* by Vickie McDonough?
   ❑ Very much! I would like to see more books by this author!
   ❑ Moderately. I would have enjoyed it more if

   _____

   _____

   _____

2. Are you a member of **Heartsong Presents**? ❑ Yes ❑ No
   If no, where did you purchase this book? _____

   _____

3. How would you rate, on a scale from 1 (poor) to 5 (superior), the cover design? _____

4. On a scale from 1 (poor) to 10 (superior), please rate the following elements.

   ____ Heroine   ____ Plot
   ____ Hero   ____ Inspirational theme
   ____ Setting   ____ Secondary characters

5. These characters were special because? _____

_____

_____

6. How has this book inspired your life? _____

_____

_____

7. What settings would you like to see covered in future
   Heartsong Presents books? _____

_____

_____

8. What are some inspirational themes you would like to see
   treated in future books? _____

_____

_____

9. Would you be interested in reading other **Heartsong
   Presents** titles? ❑ Yes ❑ No

10. Please check your age range:
       ❑ Under 18   ❑ 18-24
       ❑ 25-34   ❑ 35-45
       ❑ 46-55   ❑ Over 55

Name _____

Occupation _____

Address _____

City, State, Zip _____

The
Spinster Brides
OF CACTUS CORNER

4 stories in 1

Unmarried women committed to helping orphaned children in their community aren't necessarily looking for love when romance sweeps into their small Arizona town.

Frances Devine, Lena Nelson Dooley, Vickie McDonough, and Jeri Odell share the stories of four spinster Arizonans who happen upon love in the midst of an orphanage ministry.

Historical, paperback, 352 pages, 5³/₁₆" x 8"

Heart♥ong

**Any 12
Heartsong
Presents titles
for only
$27.00***

HISTORICAL
ROMANCE IS CHEAPER
BY THE DOZEN!

Buy any assortment of twelve
Heartsong Presents **titles and save**
25% off of the already discounted
price of $2.97 each!

*plus $3.00 shipping and handling per order
and sales tax where applicable.
If outside the U.S. please call
740-922-7280 for shipping charges.

HEARTSONG PRESENTS TITLES AVAILABLE NOW:

___HP483 *Forever Is Not Long Enough,*
      B. Youree
___HP484 *The Heart Knows,* E. Bonner
___HP488 *Sonoran Sweetheart,* N. J. Farrier
___HP491 *An Unexpected Surprise,* R. Dow
___HP495 *With Healing in His Wings,*
      S. Krueger
___HP496 *Meet Me with a Promise,* J. A. Grote
___HP500 *Great Southland Gold,* M. Hawkins
___HP503 *Sonoran Secret,* N. J. Farrier
___HP507 *Trunk of Surprises,* D. Hunt
___HP511 *To Walk in Sunshine,* S. Laity
___HP512 *Precious Burdens,* C. M. Hake
___HP515 *Love Almost Lost,* I. B. Brand
___HP519 *Red River Bride,* C. Coble
___HP520 *The Flame Within,* P. Griffin
___HP523 *Raining Fire,* L. A. Coleman
___HP524 *Laney's Kiss,* T. V. Bateman
___HP531 *Lizzie,* L. Ford
___HP535 *Viking Honor,* D. Mindrup
___HP536 *Emily's Place,* T. V. Bateman
___HP539 *Two Hearts Wait,* F. Chrisman
___HP540 *Double Exposure,* S. Laity
___HP543 *Cora,* M. Colvin
___HP544 *A Light Among Shadows,* T. H. Murray
___HP547 *Maryelle,* L. Ford
___HP551 *Healing Heart,* R. Druten
___HP552 *The Vicar's Daughter,* K. Comeaux
___HP555 *But for Grace,* T. V. Bateman
___HP556 *Red Hills Stranger,* M. G. Chapman
___HP559 *Banjo's New Song,* R. Dow
___HP560 *Heart Appearances,* P. Griffin
___HP563 *Redeemed Hearts,* C. M. Hake
___HP567 *Summer Dream,* M. H. Flinkman
___HP568 *Loveswept,* T. H. Murray

___HP571 *Bayou Fever,* K. Y'Barbo
___HP575 *Kelly's Chance,* W. E. Brunstetter
___HP576 *Letters from the Enemy,* S. M. Warren
___HP579 *Grace,* L. Ford
___HP580 *Land of Promise,* C. Cox
___HP583 *Ramshackle Rose,* C. M. Hake
___HP584 *His Brother's Castoff,* L. N. Dooley
___HP587 *Lilly's Dream,* P. Darty
___HP588 *Torey's Prayer,* T. V. Bateman
___HP591 *Eliza,* M. Colvin
___HP592 *Refining Fire,* C. Cox
___HP599 *Double Deception,* L. Nelson Dooley
___HP600 *The Restoration,* C. M. Hake
___HP603 *A Whale of a Marriage,* D. Hunt
___HP604 *Irene,* L. Ford
___HP607 *Protecting Amy,* S. P. Davis
___HP608 *The Engagement,* K. Comeaux
___HP611 *Faithful Traitor,* J. Stengl
___HP612 *Michaela's Choice,* L. Harris
___HP615 *Gerda's Lawman,* L. N. Dooley
___HP616 *The Lady and the Cad,* T. H. Murray
___HP619 *Everlasting Hope,* T. V. Bateman
___HP620 *Basket of Secrets,* D. Hunt
___HP623 *A Place Called Home,* J. L. Barton
___HP624 *One Chance in a Million,* C. M. Hake
___HP627 *He Loves Me, He Loves Me Not,*
      R. Druten
___HP628 *Silent Heart,* B. Youree
___HP631 *Second Chance,* T. V. Bateman
___HP632 *Road to Forgiveness,* C. Cox
___HP635 *Hogtied,* L. A. Coleman
___HP636 *Renegade Husband,* D. Mills
___HP639 *Love's Denial,* T. H. Murray
___HP640 *Taking a Chance,* K. E. Hake
___HP643 *Escape to Sanctuary,* M. J. Conner

(If ordering from this page, please remember to include it with the order form.)